# TRIGGER WARNING

## ALLAN LEVERONE

**TRIGGER WARNING**

Copyright ©2014 by Allan Leverone

Cover artwork and design by Elderlemon Design
Print edition formatting by JD Smith Design

# 1

"I'm wondering if you've ever spent any time considering the subject of irony." Jack Sheridan stopped what he was doing and glanced at his companion for the evening.

No answer.

The man returned Jack's gaze, his eyes angry and smoldering—and perhaps a little afraid—above his gagged and taped mouth. A verbal response at this point seemed unlikely.

Jack shrugged. "I didn't think so," he said as he finished drilling a series of pilot holes into the surface of a sturdy wooden workbench.

He placed the drill to the side and picked up a screwdriver. "You don't strike me as the introspective type, what with your affinity for blowing up innocent people under the guise of radical Islamic jihad."

He placed a hastily constructed iron frame over the pilot holes and began screwing down the base, taking his time to ensure a secure fit. "Oh, I don't doubt you've convinced yourself you are 'justified' in taking innocent lives and terrorizing people who've never done a damned thing to you or the lunatics you represent."

The screwdriver went next to the electric drill on the workbench and Jack grasped the frame with both hands, manipulating it to test his work. It featured a wide footing, with a thick, two-foot-high metal pipe spiking straight up off the base. An inch below the top, Jack had drilled a pair of holes into the pipe.

The contraption was rudimentary. Jack had never paid much

attention in metal shop as a kid, and he'd been out of school a long time. But his creation seemed solid, and unless he missed his guess it would serve its purpose well.

And that was all he cared about.

"Let's face it," he continued, locking eyes with the man sitting bound and gagged just a few feet away. "You're not the sharpest knife in the drawer, anyway, are you Muhammad?"

The man blinked in surprise and Jack smiled. "That's right, I know your name. Muhammad Abadi. I know a lot about you, Muhammad. As my mother used to say, you were stuck at the end of the line when they were handing out brains, weren't you?"

Abadi's eyes darkened and Jack continued. "There's no shame in that, by the way. There are plenty of people in the world a hell of a lot smarter than me. But really, Muhammad, couldn't you have at least tried to show a *little* originality? I mean, blowing up a pressure-cooker bomb at the finish line of the New York City Marathon seems so…passé, don't you agree?"

He shook his head in mock confusion. "Been there, done that, am I right? And you must have seen how everything played out for your brothers-in-arms in Boston. Those guys weren't the sharpest knives either, and they didn't last very long after *their* short time in the limelight, did they?"

He picked up a small wireless remote control device that featured a single red plastic button and began securing it to the top of the metal pipe, using a pair of thin but strong wire cables. Abadi's forehead wrinkled as his concern began to grow, and Jack guessed he had by now figured out the gist of what was happening here.

By the look on his face, he didn't seem to like it much.

Good.

"I know what you're thinking," Jack said as he slipped the cable through each of the holes he'd drilled in the pipe and wound it around the inside several times before feeding it out the other side.

He spoke chummily as he worked, just one stranger chatting to another. Passing the time. "You're wondering how the hell I was able to find you when the police, the FBI, DHS, and all those other alphabet-soup agencies have been whiffing on you for months."

Penetrating stare from Abadi.

"Here's the thing, my fanatical friend. As even someone of your limited intelligence has undoubtedly determined by now, I do not represent traditional law enforcement. In fact, I don't represent law enforcement at all."

He picked up a welder's mask and slipped it over his head, then lifted a welding torch and lit it. He began securing the wire cable to the pipe. A moment later he extinguished the torch and removed the mask, then placed it neatly next to the drill and the screwdriver on the workbench.

"You see, Muhammad, my employers are not subject to the limitations imposed on law enforcement agencies within the United States. What's more, they're privy to avenues of information unavailable to those in official positions. And that information is almost always accurate, particularly in cases like yours."

Jack grasped the remote and began tugging on it, testing his welding skills.

"The fact of the matter is, Muhammad, you're not very well liked, even among the local scumbag population. It was not a difficult task to get people—the kind of people who would never talk to the police or FBI in a million years—to spill their guts to us."

The cable seemed to be holding, so he pulled harder. It was critical Abadi not be able to free the remote from the pipe, and he would soon be highly motivated to do exactly that.

"And I hate to have to break this to you, Muhammad." He lowered his voice and spoke conspiratorially. "Slimeballs were falling all over themselves to give you up. They were like teenage girls storming the stage at a One Direction concert. Hell, we had so many informants we had to turn them away after awhile. You may have thought you were operating in secret, but this neighborhood is actually quite tight-knit. It's hard to hide everything from everyone, Muhammad, as I suppose even you must have concluded by now."

He yanked with all the leverage he could muster against the cable and it showed no sign of snapping. Finally he nodded in satisfaction and turned his attention back to his prisoner.

"Looks like everything's set for the main event. Before we get started, though, weren't we discussing something important, getting to know each other a little, before I got sidetracked onto the subject of how badly you fucked up by killing all those innocent people?"

3

Abadi was breathing heavily now, no longer even attempting to hide his fear. That distress didn't seem to have lessened his hatred for Jack, though. His eyes were every bit as angry now as they had been when Jack jammed the barrel of a gun in his ear on the sidewalk below the makeshift bomb factory Abadi had set up inside an abandoned tenement building.

"Oh, I remember now," Jack said, snapping his fingers. "We were discussing the concept of irony. Since our little bullshit session seems to be running low on time, I'll get right to the point. It's ironic that the method you chose to murder nearly a dozen innocent people during the marathon has made it so easy for me to exact vengeance on you."

Angry glare.

"I mean, if not for the delicious irony, I would probably have had to use three different backpacks or a large equipment bag to haul all the tools up here that I needed to do this." He nodded at the contraption he'd fabricated.

"And I gotta be honest, Muhammad. You're really not worth that kind of effort."

Jack stood and moved behind the chair into which he'd strapped Muhammad Abadi. He tilted it back and slid it across the dirty floor until the terrorist was positioned directly in front of the workbench upon which Jack had secured the wireless remote. The device hung from the top of the pipe by the two inches of play Jack had left in the cable.

"Do me a favor," he said, his tone almost—but not quite—friendly. "See if you can reach that."

Abadi shook his head defiantly.

"Suit yourself." Jack reached down and grabbed the terrorist's hands, which were secured together at the wrists. He yanked them forward. He'd tied the man's arms to the back of the chair above the elbow and Abadi gasped in pain.

"Perfect," Jack said with a grim smile. There was just enough play in the heavy twine he'd used on Abadi's arms to permit the man to reach the remote dangling from the top of the pipe.

He released the terrorist's hands and moved to a pressure cooker he'd placed at the end of the workbench. Slid it across the bench until it was positioned next to the remote, but out of Abadi's reach.

"In case you've forgotten, or were so humiliated by the ease with which I corralled such a supposedly dangerous terrorist that you can't think straight," Jack said, "let me remind you that I've packed this pressure cooker with exactly the items you used to wreak such havoc at the marathon finish line. Nails, screws, bolts, shards of glass."

He glanced down at the man. "Let's not beat around the bush, shall we, Muhammad? You know, since we've become so close and all."

Abadi didn't answer.

Jack took his silence as agreement that, yes, they had become close. "The cooker is packed full of shrapnel. And we both know the kind of damage shrapnel can do to fragile human bodies, don't we?"

This time Abadi's glare contained equal portions of hatred and fear.

He pretended not to notice as he continued speaking. "I believe we're now ready to begin. And to make things interesting, I'm going to give you an opportunity I'm sure you're not expecting."

Abadi's forehead wrinkled in confusion. Jack knew he had already guessed his fate, but this curveball threw him for a loop.

"I know you're a religious fanatic," Jack continued. "The fact that your little personal *jihad* killed a dozen people makes that abundantly clear. So, given your deeply held religious convictions, I'm going to offer you the chance, right here and now, to avail yourself of those seventy-six virgins that seem so important to you people. And as a bonus, you can remove your killer—that's me, in case you haven't been paying attention—from the face of the earth as well."

Jack grabbed Abadi's hands again and lifted them to the remote. They were shaking badly and he grinned. "Your body betrays you," he said.

He placed the remote in Abadi's hands, forcing the man's thumb to depress the red button in its center. Then he reached down and flipped a switch he'd mounted on the side of the pressure cooker. The action activated the wireless radio receiver packed inside next to the C4 charge and the shrapnel.

"As I'm sure even you have guessed by now," Jack said, "the

device I've constructed is a dead-man's switch. I'm not too proud to admit my work doesn't come close to matching the electronic artistry of yours, but then I haven't had as much practice as you in the art of bomb-making, have I, Muhammad?"

The remote jiggled as Abadi clutched it desperately, his uplifted arms stretched to their limit. "But my work, although admittedly simplistic, accomplishes my objective. As long as you continue to depress the red button on the remote, you're perfectly safe. And, of course, by extension, so am I. The moment you stop pressing that button, though, or let go of the remote, well, I guess we both know what's going to happen then."

Abadi's arms were beginning to shake worse, and Jack wondered whether it was out of fear or from the strain of keeping his arms raised tautly against the restraints. If he lowered them even two inches, he would lose contact with the remote.

"So here's the deal, Mr. Dedicated Islamic Terrorist. All you need do to avail yourself of the virgins awaiting you, and to take me along for the ride, is to let go of that button. Seems to me it should be an easy decision for such a committed jihadist as yourself."

He waited next to Abadi's chair. His heart was racing and adrenaline pounded through his system, but he forced calmness into his voice and nonchalance into his posture.

"Well? What are you waiting for?"

Abadi's arms began to spasm, but Jack noticed his death grip on the remote hadn't wavered.

"Yeah," he said, nodding. "I thought the events of the last few minutes might have shifted your priorities a little."

Jack patted Abadi on the shoulder almost pleasantly. "That's all I wanted to know. Good luck holding on," he said. "Maybe if you can stay alive long enough, one of your accomplices will walk in here and get you out of this mess."

He strolled toward the door, then turned and faced the terrorist one last time.

"Oh, that's right," he said. "You had no accomplices. You're one of those lone wolves we're supposed to be so afraid of. Bad break for you, I guess."

Jack walked through the door and closed it securely behind him.

Descended the rickety stairs and walked out the abandoned tenement building into the bright Bronx sunshine.

Walked down the trash-littered alley toward the street.

Made it almost halfway before the sound of the explosion reached his ears.

# 2

Bradley Chilcott sat in the semi-darkness of his home study, telephone in one hand and whiskey tumbler in the other. He rarely looked forward to phone calls but had been eagerly anticipating this one all day.

At work, even his chief of staff had even noticed he was on pins and needles. "Sir, you look exactly like a nine-year-old on Christmas Eve."

He'd laughed the comment off and gone about his business—not that the fucking Lieutenant Governor of fucking Maryland ever had particularly pressing business to attend to, anyway—but the fact of the matter was, Doreen's observation had been right on the money. He *did* feel like a kid on Christmas Eve.

Bradley's chief of security, Mike Hargus, was out of state on "non-official" official business and he would be reporting in today. It was a trip that would play a critical role in Bradley realizing his long-held goal of winning the presidency of the United States, so his anxiety made perfect sense.

It was also dangerous and risky. It was the kind of operation that could—and likely *would*—land him in jail if it went sideways.

But jobs like this were exactly the reason Bradley had hired his own private security man rather than utilizing the Maryland State Police on the rare occasions protection was necessary. Hargus was ex-CIA. He was tough and efficient and discreet. He knew how to do the dirty work and keep his mouth shut afterward.

Hargus had been with Bradley since before Bradley's first

campaign for elective office, and if everything went according to plan, he would accompany Bradley all the way to the Oval Office. Because Bradley knew that if a pissant lieutenant governor needed the kind of services provided by a man like Mike Hargus, the president of the United States would need them even more.

The *reason* Bradley was so anxious to receive tonight's phone call was because he'd painted himself into a goddamned corner; something he'd never imagined possible.

Back when he was no more than ten, young Bradley Chilcott had sat down at his pressboard desk in his basement bedroom and composed an action plan, a chart detailing the steps he believed it would take to become the most powerful man in the world.

Most young boys played sports and dreamed of sex with their teachers. Bradley Chilcott lusted for power and influence, and the resulting wealth that power and influence would attract.

So he'd codified his plan: earn outstanding grades, graduate high school as valedictorian, attend an exclusive university with a Political Science major. Seek out and marry an attractive and intelligent woman. Work on political campaigns, first as an intern and then later as paid staff, gaining valuable experience before putting that experience to use in the political arena in his own right.

As time passed, Bradley had of course rewritten and amended his action plan. Even the most insightful ten-year-old could not possibly foresee the myriad ways his life would be affected by events beyond his control. But for the most part, the chart he'd spent so much time constructing as a young boy had guided his life and career with precision and accuracy.

Straight A's in high school, along with participation in sports and student government. A Political Science major at Georgetown University and an impressive 4.0 GPA, followed by an MBA in Government.

He was able to check the box on his action plan involving the acquisition of a wife while a student at Georgetown as well. Kim was blonde, beautiful and smart as a whip. She was perfect.

The two made a formidable and photogenic pair. Bradley was ruggedly handsome, with a square jaw, steel grey hair and movie star looks—maybe he wasn't leading-man material, but he was certainly supporting-actor worthy—that translated well to television screens, which was of course a critical piece of the modern political puzzle.

Kim Chilcott was petite and equally photogenic, with electric blue eyes and a dazzling smile she could summon at any time and under any circumstances. And although she was intelligent—in moments of self-reflection Bradley had to admit his wife was probably smarter than he—she had no particular craving for the limelight, in direct opposition to Bradley's personality. She was comfortable in the public eye, but there was no danger of her ever upstaging her husband. At least not on purpose.

In short, she was the ideal political wife. Bradley wasn't sure he loved her; hell, he wasn't sure he was capable of actually *loving* anyone other than himself.

But that was beside the point. He got along with Kim well enough, provided she toed the line, and she projected a certain veneer of respectability—the All-American Girl—that was every bit as important as good looks for achieving success in the American political system.

After receiving their masters' degrees, Bradley and Kim had struck out on the path prescribed by Bradley's action plan. The pair took an apartment in Washington, D.C. and began working for senators with radically divergent leanings: Bradley for a liberal Democrat from Massachusetts and Kim for a conservative Republican from Georgia.

The philosophical inclinations of their bosses were irrelevant. What mattered was gaining the experience and contacts a political career would require.

After several years, Kim left the workforce when she became pregnant with the first of a pair of Chilcott boys, and Bradley moved on to a job at the CIA in the administration of the newly elected U.S. president, who'd been backed both financially and politically by the very influential senator from Massachusetts.

After ten years at the CIA, during which he'd developed the kind of contacts most power-hungry politicians could only dream about, Bradley and Kim returned home to Maryland to take the next step in the grand plan.

It was here Bradley made the mistake that would lead directly to today's telephone call he was so anxiously anticipating. Finally prepared to begin his long-awaited run to the White House, Bradley took his first shot at elective office, announcing his candidacy for lieutenant governor of Maryland and aligning himself with the eventual winner in the gubernatorial election, Jim Studds.

The pairing was perfect from Bradley's point of view. The Democrat Studds was a highly visible and popular ex-prosecuting attorney who would have no trouble winning votes and who was facing a weak opponent. And the best part was that he was old. Nearing seventy at the time of the election three years ago, Studds had made it clear to Bradley he was interested in one term only, then retirement to his estate in the Maryland countryside.

Bradley would then be in line to move to the governor's mansion.

Perfect.

But there was one problem.

And it was a big one.

Bradley Chilcott's political career was in danger of running straight into a brick wall. A dead end before it had even really gotten started.

Because Jim Studds had changed his mind about retirement. He advised Bradley just a few weeks ago that his health was good and he loved being governor and rather than retire after one term he'd decided to run for reelection next year.

Of course, he would love it if Bradley would team up with him again.

As lieutenant governor.

And that was unacceptable.

It was more than a year until the election, and then assuming the ticket was victorious—and it would be—another four years would pass with Bradley stuck in his current useless, pointless, career-ending position.

Five years from now, the contacts Bradley had worked so hard to attain would be ancient. Worthless. All of them, at the CIA, the Department of State, in the White House and the administrations of key battleground national election states, they would all be cold as ice. Most of them would have moved on and forgotten Bradley Chilcott ever existed.

The implications for Bradley's action plan were obvious and

chilling. He would have wasted virtually his entire adult life. His political career would be as good as finished, and now in his mid-forties he was far too old to start over.

Besides, his action plan included no provision for a reboot.

No provision for failure.

Bradley had given plenty of thought to potential responses to Jim Studds' shocking announcement in the weeks since being caught completely off-guard. It would not be inaccurate to say that those potential responses were *all* he'd been thinking about.

And after those awful first few days, when he'd wallowed in anger and despair and self-pity—and allowed himself to blow off steam by beating Kim even worse and more often than usual—Bradley Chilcott had done what he always did: he rebounded. He amended his action plan to deal with Studds' stunning betrayal.

The first step in his updated plan had been to send Mike Hargus on assignment. This afternoon's highly anticipated telephone call would—hopefully—set that updated action plan into motion.

And Bradley could hardly wait.

# 3

So far, the call wasn't going the way he'd hoped. Bradley's mood was darkening as his anger seethed.

He'd selected the target for Hargus's reconnaissance very carefully, and after serious deliberation. He pored over files he'd liberated from the CIA during his tenure at the agency, smuggled out because he'd anticipated a time when he might require certain services so discreet and dangerous even Hargus could not handle them.

After making his selection he'd verified through one of his remaining contacts at the agency that his choice was a good one for what he had in mind. Speaking hypothetically and off the record, of course.

And now Hargus was on the other end of the line, telling Bradley there was some sort of "unanticipated situation."

Bradley sighed heavily. Unanticipated situation.

"English, Mike. Speak English, for chrissakes. What's the problem?"

"I wouldn't say it's a problem, exactly. Just something I hadn't expected based on our intel regarding Sheridan."

Bradley's mood soured a bit more as he sipped his Chivas. He was having a hard time getting past Hargus's choice of wording. "Unanticipated situation."

He hated the sound of those words. They brought a bad taste to his mouth. Unanticipated situations represented risk, and the project Bradley was considering was plenty risky already.

Hargus remained silent on the other end of the line, waiting for Bradley to ask the obvious question instead of just volunteering the information like he should. Asshole.

"Well?" Bradley barked. "Are you going to explain what the hell you're talking about or do I have to guess like a goddamn carnival psychic?"

"There's a woman."

"A woman? What are you talking about? What woman?" Everything Bradley knew about Jack Sheridan—and it was a lot— suggested the man was eminently aware of the risk posed by the nature of his work, and unwilling to expose innocent lives to that risk by involving himself in any significant way with any woman.

"Her name is Edie Tolliver. She owns a small restaurant near Sheridan's home."

"What makes you think they're together? Maybe they're just friends. Not everyone's an antisocial loner like you, you know."

"Point taken. But based on what I saw at Tolliver's diner a few days ago, if they're friends it's one hell of an intimate friendship. I thought they were going to clear off a table and get busy in front of the whole restaurant."

"Well," Bradley said thoughtfully. He sipped his drink and stroked his chin. "Isn't that interesting?"

He'd known almost from the moment his new action plan began to take shape that Jack Sheridan was the man for the job. His skill set was perfectly suited to the task he had in mind. Sure, Bradley had done his due diligence and considered other opera- tors. It would have been foolish not to. But he'd always known he would come back to Sheridan.

And in the end he had.

There was only one problem, and it was a doozy: there was no way in the world Sheridan would agree to carry out the assign- ment. Bradley had been so certain of that fact he almost didn't even bother sending Hargus to New Hampshire.

But shrinking violets didn't succeed in the political arena, and Bradley possessed a supreme confidence in his ability to get the job done. So he'd decided to begin surveillance on Sheridan and then try to figure a way to convince the man to do his bidding when the time came.

There was always a way.

And, as usual, Bradley's intuition seemed to have been proven correct. If the news about a woman in Sheridan's life was accurate, it could be a game-changer. Because a man with nothing to lose is a man you cannot control. Threatening someone like Jack Sheridan directly, he knew, would be…counterproductive.

Not to mention, in all probability, deadly.

But a man with emotional ties, especially when those ties were to a woman, was a different story. That man could be manipulated. Controlled.

Convinced—*okay, forced*, Bradley admitted to himself—to do things he would never otherwise consider.

Reprehensible things.

Things exactly like what Bradley Chilcott had in mind.

This telephone call had gone nothing at all like Bradley had expected. But rather than being filled with bad news, as he'd feared when Hargus started talking, it had taken a promising turn. A very promising turn.

"And there's more," Hargus said.

"More? Like what?"

"The Tolliver woman has a child. A seven-year-old daughter."

"A child."

"That's right."

"Seven years old."

"Yes."

*Game-changer indeed*, Bradley thought as he drained his Chivas.

# 4

Janie Tolliver screamed. The sound was loud and piercing, and when she stopped she did so only long enough to draw in a deep breath and scream again.

Then she burst out laughing.

Jack was laughing as well as he held the girl by the wrists and helicoptered her in a circle, her feet suspended in the air and her blonde pigtails streaming behind her like tiny propellers.

Eventually he lost his balance and collapsed in a heap. The little girl landed next to him and rolled through the thick grass, a victim of her momentum.

Next to them Edie Tolliver grinned. "Had enough yet?"

Jack looked up at the pretty young woman who at the moment was spinning against the backdrop of the sky. "Which one of us are you talking to?"

"The one who's supposed to be an adult."

"Oh-oh," Jack said to Janie in a conspiratorial stage whisper. "I think you're in trouble."

Janie burst out in a fit of giggles and Edie shook her head. "I'm pretty sure you're only dating me so you can play with my daughter and roll around in the grass and act like a little kid. Any truth to that?"

"I can neither confirm nor deny," he said and rolled away as she pretended to aim a kick at his head.

"Okay, okay," he said, raising his hands in mock surrender. "The truth is, I enjoy playing with you, too. Just wait until the world stops spinning, you're going to get the same treatment as Janie."

"Yeah, yeah, do it!" the little girl shouted and crawled toward them on her hands and knees.

The trio had spent the afternoon at a movie, and then gone to an early dinner followed by a trip to Janie's favorite playground. The sun had by now almost fully set and even in May, evenings tended to get chilly in New Hampshire. The ground had begun to cool and was leaching the heat out of Jack's body where he lay. He knew Janie must be getting cold in her light jacket, but she would never admit to it while having so much fun.

He climbed to his feet, brushing the dirt and grass off his clothes and helping Janie do the same.

"I think your mom's helicopter ride is going to have to wait until next time," he told her ruefully. "It's getting late. I know you have school tomorrow so it's important to get you home before bedtime."

She scuffed at the ground with the toe of one dirty sneaker and he smiled.

"Besides," he added. "Your mom's pretty old. We wouldn't want her to fall and break a hip or anything."

Edie rabbit-punched his shoulder as Janie dissolved in another fit of giggles.

They walked slowly toward the parking lot and it occurred to Jack that the petite blonde woman's playful comment about his relationship with her daughter really wasn't that far off the mark.

He adored everything about Edie, from her seemingly unlimited energy in restoring her business after her husband had walked out on her and their young child, to her bubbly personality and good humor, to her straightforwardness, to her breathtaking natural beauty.

Jack had known her for years as owner of his favorite restaurant, The Three Squares Diner, but only very recently had they begun dating. And already he suspected he was falling head-over-heels for her. He wasn't someone who'd had a lot of experience with relationships, so he couldn't say for certain *what* he was feeling.

But it sure felt a lot like love.

And what was more, he knew she felt the same way about him. The proof was walking along right next to them: Edie was fiercely protective of her daughter and would never have considered allowing Janie to start getting close to a man she wasn't serious about.

Having said all that, he really did enjoy spending time with little Janie Tolliver. She'd gotten a raw deal from her father, and Jack knew that as badly as Edie had been hurt by the man's cowardly disappearance, the effect on Janie had been worse. If Jack could help remove her lingering pain, even if only slightly and for a little while, he was happy to do so.

And he loved seeing the world through the innocent eyes of a seven-year-old. How she could look at an ordinary cloud and see not water vapor but rather a lion or a dragon or a medieval fortress.

How she could pick a dandelion out of a field of a thousand dandelions that all looked exactly the same, then shield and protect it during a walk before finally presenting it to her mother after they'd returned home.

How she could ask an endless litany of questions on any subject, all of them perfectly sensible through the lens of a child's experience. How she was never satisfied with a pat answer to those questions and would continue to badger the adult until receiving a response that made sense to her.

He especially loved how that trait drove Edie crazy.

The more time he spent in their company, the more fascinated he became by the striking similarities between mother and daughter. The way they both chewed on the corners of their lower lips when they were lost in concentration. The way they both threw back their heads and laughed when something struck them as funny.

The similarities were simultaneously eerie and captivating.

But the biggest reason he so enjoyed including Janie in his time with Edie was simple. He'd spent his entire adult life alone and he was sick of it. One-night stands during his time overseas in the military, and random hookups as he crisscrossed the country performing his unique duties for The Organization became much less satisfying the older he got.

Sex was wonderful.

Sex without companionship and emotion and tenderness was starting to seem pointless.

So while Jack treasured his time with Edie, and was careful to plan events for just the two of them, he relished including Janie whenever possible. The girl's outsized personality never failed to bring a smile to his face, and lightness to a heart that had grown increasingly heavy with all he'd seen and done over the years. And although she had never spoken of it, Jack knew Edie appreciated his unreserved affection—hell, maybe love would be an accurate description here, too—for her little girl.

Jack's longtime fear of exposing someone he cared about to undue risk had never faded, and he knew it never would. Given his career choice, it could be no other way. But as time passed, he found that the desire for companionship and family was beginning to override his concerns about security.

After all, The Organization was so secretive, so shadowy, only a handful of people in the entire country were even aware of its existence. They were powerful, rich and influential people, to be sure, but there were still only a few of them. And they had as much to lose as Jack—or any other Organization operative—should the existence of the group ever become public knowledge.

As a result, Organization management protected the identities of their members zealously. Security was their prime consideration, yesterday, today and always. Thus the odds of Jack's Organization status ever putting those close to him at risk were minimal, unless his own actions during an assignment compromised his personal security.

Thus, provided he remained vigilant—and he knew he would—there should be no reason why he couldn't have the companionship, and eventually maybe even the family, he craved while still keeping those closest to him safe.

It was doable.

It was definitely doable.

*　*　*

The temperature continued to drop as the sun settled below the horizon. Janie's reluctance to leave the playground was obvious and she dawdled, despite the fact she was beginning to shiver under her jacket.

Edie was alternately coaxing and threatening in her attempts to move the little girl along, and Jack could sense her mounting frustration.

He bugged his eyes out and turned toward Janie. Began walking stiff-legged in her direction like a zombie and in as spooky a voice as he could manage, said, "We need to hurry, it's getting cooooold out."

Janie laughed and screamed at the same time and sprinted off in the direction of the parking lot.

Jack grinned and waggled his eyebrows at Edie, then took off behind the girl.

He yelled, "I'll bet if we're really good on the ride home, your mom will make us some hot chocolate!"

Janie turned around and answered, "I bet she will!" before resuming her all-out sprint toward the truck.

Moments later, Edie touched Jack on the elbow as he was lifting Janie into the truck. "That's not fair, Mister. I don't have any choice about the hot chocolate now."

He winked. "I don't play fair. I thought you knew that."

They climbed into the truck and drove off toward Edie's home.

# 5

Kim Chilcott twirled a stray lock of hair with her finger as she loitered outside the closed door of her husband's home office.

The hair thing was a nervous habit she'd never realized she had until after the first time Bradley assaulted her. That revelation—that her husband was a sociopathic monster—had occurred years ago, not long after the birth of their first child, but Kim could still recall every last detail of that awful day as if it had just happened.

She doubted the clarity would ever fade.

They'd been fighting. The subject of their disagreement was the same thing young couples had struggled with since the beginning of time: money. Bradley was convinced Kim spent too much of it. He felt she wasted his hard-earned cash on unnecessary extravagances.

Like groceries and the heating bill.

The ironic part of the whole heated "discussion" was that the money in question belonged every bit as much to Kim as it did Bradley. She was still working at the time, earning roughly the same salary as her husband. Hell, she was probably making more. She certainly worked harder.

That hadn't mattered to Bradley, of course. Nothing but Bradley's opinion ever mattered to Bradley. He'd become increasingly agitated as they sniped back and forth across the dinner table, eventually losing himself in his fury, pushing to his feet and slapping her.

The fight itself was nothing serious, really, aside from what it represented. Kim had grown up with two older brothers who enjoyed nothing more than torturing their little sister as she struggled to keep up. Both of them had smacked her harder on numerous occasions than Bradley's little dinner table girlie-slap.

But Bradley Chilcott was nothing if not a quick learner, and within a couple of months he'd hit her again. This time the blow was harder.

More menacing.

More damaging.

And it was deliberate. It wasn't a momentary slip-up in the heat of an argument, followed immediately—as the first one had been—by shame-faced apologies and assurances nothing of the kind would ever happen again.

Even at the time, Kim wasn't so sure she could believe her husband's words. She'd suspected the first assault was intentional.

But suspicions were unnecessary the second time. He'd *meant* to do it. Even now, years later, with the weight of experience behind her, Kim had a hard time wrapping her mind around that fact. Bradley had gotten angry—not even at Kim, except peripherally—and he'd struck her again.

And this time his assault was more cunning, as if he'd pre-planned after the first time how he was going to attack his wife when he got angry enough to do it again.

He didn't hit her in the face like he had on that first shocking occasion. Cheeks bruised easily and a nose could be broken in an instant. Either occurrence would be difficult to explain away and could be a career-ender for a man with his eyes fixed on a national political career.

Instead, he punched her in the stomach. Three hard blows that buckled Kim at the waist and sucked the breath out of her lungs. She was left gasping for air and sobbing on the kitchen floor while her husband stalked away.

His apology came later that night and felt utterly insincere to Kim, as if he couldn't even be bothered to maintain the fiction that he'd simply gotten carried away in the heat of the moment.

The next assault came just weeks later and featured kicks and punches to her buttocks.

And just like that Kim Chilcott became a walking, talking

cliché: the helpless domestic assault victim, unable to escape her attacker because she needed to keep her children safe, and let's face it: there was no way on God's green earth she would be able to match Bradley's resources in a custody battle. She'd been raised in upper-middle-class comfort, but he'd grown up with a silver spoon planted firmly in his mouth.

If it came down to a battle of finances, she would lose.

In the years since that first horrifying realization her husband was not the man she thought she knew, nearly every inch of Kim's body that could be covered up with clothing or otherwise hidden from view had been damaged by her husband's inability to control his temper. His childish petulance. His smoldering rage.

Kim would never have imagined she could fall victim to domestic violence. The daughter of an enlightened father and a feminist mother, Kim would have counseled any abused spouse to walk away, to file a restraining order against the son of a bitch immediately and then take him for everything he had.

Until the shoe had been on *her* foot.

Then she just couldn't do it.

Over the ensuing years she'd resigned herself to her situation, rationalizing her lack of action by convincing herself that for all his faults, and God knew he had plenty, Bradley had never once hit the children.

Her, yes. He'd hit her plenty.

But never the children.

Her situation was simultaneously exhausting, terrifying and humiliating, made so much worse by the fact that nobody knew. Not her mother or father—who, for all his "enlightenment," would have taken a baseball bat to Bradley's head if he'd known how Bradley was treating his little girl, Kim was sure of it—not the other wives at the health club, not Kim's best friend since childhood.

Nobody.

It was her burden to bear, and hers to bear alone.

Now Kim stood uncertainly outside Bradley's study, twirling her hair and dithering. She knew she was dithering and she hated herself for it, but Bradley simply would not abide being interrupted when he was inside his study with the door closed.

What he as doing in there, she had no idea. Maybe he was busy with official State of Maryland business. Maybe he was watching porn. Maybe he was Skyping with a mistress. Kim didn't know and didn't care. He was in there, which was a damned sight better than being out here.

At least when he was in his office he wasn't hitting her.

But there *was* a problem, and that problem was the reason she was standing outside his door frozen in uncertainty. The roast would soon be as dry as the Sahara if she left it warming in the oven much longer, and bitter experience had taught her that if there was one thing Bradley hated almost as much as being interrupted in his study, it was suffering through an over-or-undercooked dinner.

She didn't know what to do.

The sound of the kids fighting in the family room floated up the stairs and Kim wished with all her heart she could be down there listening to them scream at each other rather than up here trying to decide on an action that could well determine whether she would face the next several days without experiencing intense pain, pain that she would have to try to hide from the world.

Every second that passed without a resolution to her problem brought Kim one second closer to the next beating.

Finally she said a quick prayer—why she bothered anymore she wasn't sure; God hadn't been paying attention to the Chilcott family for quite some time as far as Kim could tell—and raised her fist and rapped on the door with her knuckles.

Very quietly.

A moment of silence followed, after which an annoyed Bradley hollered, "What?" He emphasized the "T" sound to convey his displeasure.

Kim cracked the door and stuck her head through. "I'm sorry to bother you, honey, but do you have any idea how much longer you're going to be? Dinner is ready and the children are getting hungry."

She steeled herself for his reaction, which might consist of anything from a warm smile and an "I'll be right out, then," to a screaming, spitting, fists-flying tirade that would almost—but not quite—put her in the hospital.

She held her breath, trying her hardest to maintain an air of humble servitude while her heart hammered like it was preparing to burst through her chest and the blood rushed in her ears until she thought she might pass out from the stress.

For a second his face darkened and a chill went through Kim's entire body. Then he spoke into the phone—she hadn't realized he was holding it until just now—and placed the handset quietly on the cradle.

He smiled at her, his lips twisting into something resembling a cross between a grin and a sneer. She'd seen the look many times before and wondered how in God's name a man who looked as unhinged as Bradley Chilcott had ever managed to persuade enough people to vote for him to win election to the second-highest position in Maryland state government.

Of course, he'd convinced *her* to marry him and then have two children together, so she supposed she shouldn't judge the voting public too harshly.

After hanging up the phone, Bradley shoved his desk chair back with his calves and stood. This was it. Things were either going to go very rapidly downhill, or Kim would be able to breathe easy.

For a few minutes, anyway, until her husband passed judgment on dinner.

She held her breath.

Bradley's smile was followed by, "Thank you, dear. I didn't realize it had gotten so late. Governance never sleeps, right? Hell, it never even takes a break!"

She smiled and nodded. The smile was probably too bright and the nod too quick, but if Bradley noticed, he let it pass.

She said, "Your meeting went well, then?"

He shook his head in confusion. "Meeting?"

*Dammit. Why can't you learn to keep your big mouth shut.* "Well, I noticed you were on the phone. I assumed it was a strategy meeting or something."

"Oh, that. Yes, the call went well. It went better than well, really. It was fascinating."

"Oh?" Kim had learned her lesson—again—and wasn't about to fall into the trap she'd narrowly avoided by asking any more questions.

Bradley threw an arm over her shoulders. He turned and

carefully closed the door as they exited. "Yep, fascinating. Things could be changing for the better in the career of one Bradley A. Chilcott."

Kim tried to conceal her revulsion as they strolled together toward the dining room. His arm never left her shoulder.

# 6

Mike Hargus grew steadily more concerned as he maintained surveillance on his target.

He followed Sheridan all day. Started with ninety minutes sitting outside a movie theatre with his thumb up his ass as the couple and the little girl took in the latest Disney kids' flick. Moved to the parking lot of the casual Italian joint while they ate an early dinner. Watched them cavort on the playground just before nightfall.

Nothing specific about any of the group's activities triggered Mike's concern.

It was there, nevertheless.

And why wouldn't he be worried? That damned fool Bradley Chilcott had latched onto Jack Sheridan as the answer to all his problems. Chilcott was like a Rottie with a steak bone when he made up his mind about something, as he had done regarding Sheridan: relentless.

Chilcott's plan was to manipulate Sheridan into restoring the lieutenant governor's fading dream of a White House bid. He seemed to believe Sheridan possessed magical powers or something, like the guy could just snap his fingers and eliminate people.

David Copperfield making the Brooklyn Bridge disappear.

Or was it an elephant? An airplane? Apartment building, maybe?

Mike couldn't remember. He loved magic but the damn trick had been done years ago. The point was still valid, though: Bradley

Chilcott had no fucking idea what kind of tiger he'd taken by the tail when he settled on Jack Sheridan as the solution to his Jim Studds problem.

All Bradley knew about Sheridan were words he'd read in a CIA file, words detailing the man's near-mystical ability to eliminate people in ways that appeared accidental to even the most experienced investigator or forensic team.

Sheridan could supposedly clean up any mess, and a mess was exactly what the supposedly savvy Chilcott had gotten himself into.

But Jack Sheridan was more than the sum total of a few dozen pages in a secret CIA file. Mike realized as much even if his boss didn't.

Mike wasn't laboring under any Chilcott-style delusions where Sheridan was concerned. His boss looked at Jack Sheridan and saw nothing more than a blunt instrument.

But Mike saw something completely different. Mike saw a clever, intelligent, extremely dangerous operator, a man who could turn the tables on an unwitting opponent without breaking a sweat, and then make that opponent wish he'd never been born.

And it wasn't like the plan they'd developed was a bad one, as these things went. Mike and Bradley had huddled in the lieutenant governor's home office deep into many nights over the course of several weeks, planning and discussing and refining until they'd settled on what even Mike Hargus had to admit was a relatively workable solution to the problem that threatened to derail Bradley's career.

Where the two disagreed was in the selection of the proper person to execute that solution. Bradley fell in love with Sheridan almost immediately out of the possibilities he was given, but the more information Mike uncovered, the more he felt Sheridan would be absolutely the wrong choice.

But their partnership was not an equal one. Mike had known as much from the start, years ago. Bradley was a control freak. He was unquestionably in charge, possessing veto power and the final say in all matters. Mike knew his boss well enough to know he had already made up his mind.

He *should* know Chilcott, he'd been working for him long

enough. Very early in his CIA career, Mike Hargus had come to the realization he wanted more out of life than a risky job doing dangerous work for a chain of command that would cut him loose at the first sign of peril to themselves, and would do so without a second thought.

What was more, the pay sucked, relatively speaking. If Mike was going to put his life on the line, the measly seventy grand a year he was making as a civil service drone wasn't going to cut it.

Along about the time he was having this epiphany Mike had met a young agency desk jockey named Bradley Chilcott. The two men hit it off immediately, and before long Chilcott was opening up to Mike about his goals for the future and the "action plan" he'd developed to make those goals a reality.

It had occurred to Mike that this brash young man might actually go places. But to do so, he would need someone…harder. Someone with the kind of abilities and experiences men like Bradley Chilcott simply did not have.

When Bradley broached the subject, six months into the friendship, of Mike leaving government service and coming to work for him personally, it had taken roughly three seconds of consideration for Mike to agree. His wife at the time—soon to be ex-wife—disagreed with the decision vehemently, claiming with some merit that giving up a career with benefits and a guaranteed pension and respectability to go work for a young dreamer was not the sort of choice responsible family men made.

Mike made it anyway, and divorce followed, like night after day. He wasn't happy about the way his marriage turned out, but couldn't claim to be heartbroken, either. He loved his wife—he supposed—but he loved adventure and risk-taking even more.

And an adventure it had been, with Bradley Chilcott the telegenic symbol of respectability and solid leadership, and Mike Hargus the behind-the-scenes enforcer, ready and willing to intimidate whenever possible, and to utilize physical force whenever necessary to pave the way for Chilcott's political ascent.

But while Bradley Chilcott may have been a *symbol* of respectability, the man's actual persona was anything but. His foibles kept Mike busy constantly, right from the beginning of their partnership. Much of Mike's duties involved cleaning up the messes left over from Chilcott's unusual sexual interests and the excesses derived from exercising those interests.

The lieutenant governor liked young girls.

Moreover, he liked *hitting* young girls. He got off on it.

Mike thought Chilcott was a disgusting pig who would have found himself dangling by the ankles from the roof of the tallest building in D.C. had he tried any of that sick shit on one of *his* kids, or even one of his nieces or nephews. Since he never had, however, a paycheck was a paycheck, and Mike was more than willing to take whatever action deemed necessary to facilitate Chilcott's career progression.

The girls Bradley chose for his little "rough sex" scenarios were almost always unaware of Bradley's sexual proclivities before climbing into bed with him. This led to a seemingly unending succession of families to bribe and occasionally fingers to break, all to ensure silence from the women and their families as Chilcott positioned himself for the White House.

What they'd planned this time, however, went above and beyond even the dirty tricks everyone—including the American public—had learned to expect in the rough-and-tumble world of politics and governance at the highest level.

Assuming the plan came together as outlined, two people would die.

At least two.

And if the plan *didn't* come together, the potential existed for public disgrace and life behind bars—or even the death sentence—for one scheming politician and his trusty henchman.

And that was an unacceptable outcome as far as Mike Hargus was concerned.

For his part, the damned fool Chilcott never seemed to recognize the possibility of anything less than total success. During every strategy session, Mike tried to open Chilcott's eyes, to make him see the myriad ways even a perfectly planned op could go sideways. It didn't have to be the fault of the operators at all. Random chance could knock everything apart; it happened to CIA field operatives all the fucking time.

No matter how hard he tried to open Chilcott's eyes, though, Mike's boss would simply smile his stupid serene smile and say something like, "I believe in you, Mike. You just have to believe in yourself."

Damned fool. Maybe that positivity horseshit worked in the insular domain of politics, but Mike knew it was nothing more than whistling past the graveyard in the real world. Chilcott could take his hippy-dippy crap and shove it right up his ass. Protecting oneself was all about being prepared to do whatever was necessary, not being lulled into a false sense of security with a bunch of optimistic bullshit completely unmoored from reality.

And one thing Mike had learned during his CIA days kicking around shitholes like Iraq and Afghanistan was to *always* protect himself.

The moment he'd sensed which way the wind was blowing with Chilcott's plan, he'd known instinctively it was time to develop his *own* plan.

A backup plan.

A plan that would safeguard Mike Hargus's ass should everything go to hell. Lieutenant Governor Bradley Chilcott wasn't out on the front lines getting his hands dirty, which meant Chilcott could claim plausible deniability: "Your honor, *I* certainly had no idea the lengths Mr. Hargus would go to advance my political career. Why, *I* was perfectly happy being lieutenant governor. *I* never suspected the man would run afoul of the *law* in my name. I'm as shocked by Mr. Hargus's actions as you are, your honor."

Fucking asshole.

Mike felt his blood pressure rising and worked to calm himself. Hopefully things would go smoothly and Chilcott would never get the opportunity to throw Mike under the bus. But if the shit did hit the fan, Mr. Bigshot Lieutenant Governor would find the tables turned on his sorry ass before he knew what hit him.

Because Mike had secretly recorded several hours of their strategy sessions using a tiny voice-activated microcassette recorder slipped inside a shirt pocket. It was decidedly low-tech for the former CIA field operative, but was more than sufficient for Mike's purposes. He retained the recordings that incriminated his boss and eliminated the benign ones.

And now he possessed the power to destroy Chilcott.

Better yet, the man had no fucking idea. It never occurred to the boss to ensure their meetings weren't being recorded and even if it had, someone like Bradley Chilcott wouldn't have stood a snowball's chance in hell of finding the little recorder. He was a politician: soft as a marshmallow and clueless regarding operational matters. If he'd gotten a hand within twelve inches of Mike's pocket, Mike would have slapped him into next week.

As it turned out, violence—or even the threat of it—had not been necessary. Chilcott never even considered the possibility of a double-cross.

Maybe—hopefully—Mike would never have to use the tapes. Maybe—hopefully—they would remain safely inside his pocket during this operation. Mike would then transfer them to his safe-deposit box following successful completion of the op and they would never see the light of day.

But if worse came to worst, Mike Hargus would do what he'd always done—protect his own ass. In any conspiracy, law enforcement would look to utilize whatever they had on a small fish in order to land the bigger fish. Should things go sideways in this little escapade, Bradley Chilcott would represent the big fish. Mike's secret recordings would provide more than enough evidence to nail that fish to the wall, so to speak, which in turn would allow Mike to negotiate a sweet deal.

The sense of security Mike felt from having this insurance policy was palpable.

But for now, the goal was to do everything in his power to make the primary plan a success. The Chilcott gravy train was a rich one, well worth the effort and risk of keeping it on the tracks.

\* \* \*

Mike watched intently from a safe distance as Sheridan and his two women—one a petite but beautiful adult, the other a petite but adorable child—climbed into his big red Dodge Ram pickup and drove slowly out of the playground's lot. Night was falling and the lot was emptying quickly and Mike was glad he wouldn't have to hang around much longer because he would soon stick out like a sore thumb to anyone paying attention.

And Sheridan would be paying attention.

The truck turned toward town and accelerated away. Mike briefly considered following, but only briefly. If he were spotted by Sheridan everything would fall apart before it had even gotten started, and the odds that the target was going anywhere but to drop his girlfriend and her daughter at their home and then continue on to his own house were negligible.

He'd learned enough about his target anyway.

The time had come to put the plan—the primary plan, Bradley Chilcott's plan—into motion.

Mike lit a cigarette and went over the situation in his head one last time. The plan was a simple one as these things went. With his decision to seek reelection, Maryland Governor Jim Studds had positioned himself directly between Bradley Chilcott and the presidency.

Studds would thus have to be eliminated.

Since Sheridan would never agree under normal circumstances to assassinate an innocent man, he would need to be properly motivated. To properly motivate him, Mike and Bradley would need leverage.

The little girl should provide that leverage quite effectively.

Mike sat in his car, staring into the gathering darkness and thinking.

When the cigarette had burned down to a nub, he tossed it out the window and drove off in the same direction Sheridan had gone a few minutes earlier.

# 7

The car sat motionless on the side of the road, its idling engine sending a thin plume of exhaust curling into the chilly afternoon sky.

Mike Hargus sat inside, craving a cigarette and waiting for the girl to appear. He ignored the craving for now. He would need to move quickly and efficiently when little Janie Tolliver rounded the corner, and the last thing he needed was to worry about extinguishing a butt at the exact moment he should be moving his.

He'd tried to time his arrival in the neighborhood so that he wouldn't need to sit here long.

He'd done his homework and he knew where Janie Tolliver attended school.

He knew the dismissal time for that school.

He knew the little girl always walked home. Several school-aged children lived in the Tolliver's neighborhood, including a couple of older ones, and they always returned from school in a group.

They had obviously been taught to stay together. Safety in numbers and all that. Plus, this small Southern New Hampshire town was quiet and safe. Mike guessed it had been decades since the last violent crime occurred here, if ever.

From the parents' perspective, allowing the kids to walk home from school was a perfectly reasonable option.

But there was one small problem with that option, and it was a problem Mike immediately knew he could use to his advantage:

Janie Tolliver lived farther away from school than anyone else in the group. Her house was located at the end of the neighborhood cul-de-sac.

Thus the rest of the children would peel off, one by one. They would walk up their driveways and into their homes, eventually leaving Janie alone to travel the last couple hundred feet.

Undoubtedly Edie Tolliver had set up some kind of arrangement with a stay-at-home neighborhood mom to keep an eye on her child until the girl disappeared inside her house. It only made sense.

It would also fail to keep the girl safe.

Mike would need just seconds to snatch her and drive away. He'd stolen the vehicle in which he now sat, and had stolen a *second* vehicle and parked it less than a mile away. He would grab the girl, drive the short distance to the second car and hustle her into it, then drive that car away at a sedate speed, invisible and anonymous and safe.

There could be a hundred wary eyes watching the girl walk home from school, fifty people writing down the license plate number of the suspicious car sitting on the side of the road, and unless one set of those eyes belonged to an Olympic sprinter with a weapon at the ready it wasn't going to make a damned bit of difference. Janie Tolliver would be long gone before anyone even knew what the hell had happened.

That was the plan, anyway.

Mike checked his watch. He could feel a stress headache trying to take hold. This was taking too long. Time was ticking. The longer he sat here exposed, the greater the chance that something would go wrong.

He checked his watch again and muttered a curse. Maybe the little brat had stayed after school for some reason, or maybe her mother had picked her up today for a goddamned doctor's appointment, or maybe—

*Jesus Christ, settle down, you fucking pussy. You've faced Taliban fighters and Iraqi insurgents. You can handle one suburban little girl.*

He forced himself to relax. Took a deep breath. Checked his watch again; he couldn't help it, he knew he was being obsessive but—

There she was.

A small group of children rounded the corner down by the main road. They were meandering, moving slowly as children do unless the lure of ice cream is involved. The group diminished in size as it progressed until it was just Janie and one other girl.

Then the other girl veered off and Janie Tolliver waved goodbye to her and continued on.

Alone.

On a vector that would take her directly past Mike Hargus and his stolen car.

It was finally time to set this little drama in motion.

Mike leaned across the front seat, pretending to look for something in the glove box, with no idea whether the little girl was even paying the slightest attention to him. Probably she wasn't.

He monitored her progress in his peripheral vision. When she had almost reached the car, he straightened up, opened the door and stepped out onto the side of the road. He continued to ignore her.

In his hand he held a small camera, which he lifted to his face as if planning to snap a photo of something located directly over Janie Tolliver's shoulder. He began walking slowly in her direction.

She was getting concerned. He watched her through the viewfinder and could see her expression changing, morphing from carefree little girl to savvy twenty-first century child beginning to consider the Stranger Danger she'd been warned so much about but never really expected to encounter.

Still, she didn't run or scream or cross the road. Mike knew it was because he still hadn't paid any attention to her. She didn't think he even knew she was there. As far as she could see he was absorbed in taking his all-important photo of…whatever the hell was so fascinating behind her.

She was almost past him, walking more slowly but being brave and focusing on her driveway, which was less than fifty feet away.

Mike pretended to fumble with the lens. Just another second.

Now. Janie Tolliver was crossing his path.

He lowered the camera to the pocket of his trench coat and dropped it inside, then deftly removed a small zip-locked plastic bag. He unzipped the bag as she passed a couple of feet off his right, removing a rag soaked in chloroform.

He reached out and clamped the rag over the girl's mouth and nose with his right hand as his left arm encircled her waist. He pulled her tightly against him, the exact motion he would use to hug one of his kids.

She kicked and struggled and tried to scream. It was a perfectly natural reaction but exactly the wrong thing to do because it caused her to inhale deeply of the chloroform.

Within seconds she sagged limply in his arms, unconscious. Mike lifted her and carried her easily to the car. She was valuable cargo and he supported her head carefully.

The urge to look around, to see whether he was being observed, was almost overwhelming. But doing so would be pointless and cost valuable time, so he ignored it and kept going, working quickly but staying under control.

He placed her gently in the front passenger seat. Lifted a pair of handcuffs off the floor and secured her wrists behind her back, and used a second set on her ankles. Finally he clicked the seat belt into place, unsure whether it would make a damned bit of difference on an unconscious child in the event of an accident but doing so anyway.

The whole operation, from stepping out of the car to securing the girl, took less than a minute. When the girl regained consciousness—which would be fairly quickly—she would be frightened but unharmed, save for a monster of a headache.

Mike slammed the door closed and hurried around the car to the driver's side. The neighborhood seemed empty and deserted, but it was impossible to tell for sure. A frightened housewife could behind any one of those picture windows, even now dialing 911.

He dropped into the driver's seat and jammed the still-idling car into gear. Accelerated down the road and within seconds had exited the neighborhood. He turned in the direction of the second stolen car.

Five minutes later, Mike Hargus was safely lost among the speeding traffic on Interstate 93.

The snatch had gone well.

He was home free.

# 8

Jack was washing dishes when the call came in.

He'd been attempting to replicate the Western Omelets he ate several mornings a week at the Three Squares Diner, but despite several tries had been unable to come close to matching the flavor. Edie swore she'd given him her precise recipe, right down to the seasoning, but his efforts had thus far yielded disappointing—and often inedible—results.

"She's gotta be holding out on me," he muttered, tossing his frying pan into the sink in disappointment. It went against his sense of self-discipline not to wash the dirty dishes immediately, but he couldn't bring himself to face the evidence of his ongoing culinary failure.

The pan taunted him from the sink and he glared at it. "You're lucky you don't end up face-down in the dump, disloyal bastard."

When the phone rang he raised his eyebrows in surprise. He guarded his home number zealously.

Mr. Stanton, Jack's contact at The Organization, had it, of course. But as Jack had just completed the job in New York, he wasn't expecting to hear from the man for several days at least.

Besides a couple of old friends from his operator days, men to whom a telephone call on a public line was a foreign concept, the only other person he could think of who knew his number was Edie.

And it was too early for her to be out of work.

Alarm bells jangled in his head. There was no reason to feel uneasy—yet—but Jack had survived a long time in a dangerous occupation by paying close attention to a finely tuned sense of intuition. And his intuition was telling him something was…off.

He pursed his lips and dried his hands on a towel before peering at the caller ID screen. To his surprise, it was the number of the Three Squares Diner.

Edie.

He picked up the phone and kept his tone light despite the growing sensation that something must be wrong for her to call in the middle of the afternoon.

"I know there's something you're not telling me," he said. "I followed your recipe to the letter and my omelet still tasted like dirty socks. Not that I know what dirty socks taste like, mind you."

He tilted his head at the sound of a choked-off sob. The caller tried to talk and couldn't get any words out.

She tried again and failed again.

"Edie? What is it? What's the matter?"

"She's gone. M-My baby's gone."

Jack spoke softly. "Who's gone? What are you talking about?"

"Somebody took Janie. They took my little girl, Jack. Oh my God, they have my baby and—"

"Slow down, Edie, okay? Who took Janie? Tell me everything you know."

Through the line he heard a deep, shuddering breath as the woman he'd begun to fall in love with tried to get herself under control. When she resumed speaking she sounded marginally less panicked.

But only marginally.

"I've told Janie to always call me at the diner the minute she gets home from school. She does it every day, Jack. Every day. She never forgets to call."

"But today she didn't call."

"No, she didn't call. When she should have been home for ten minutes and I still hadn't heard from her, I tried calling our home phone."

"And there was no answer."

"No." Edie's voice broke and she sobbed abruptly.

"Maybe she stopped at a friend's house, or maybe she stayed after school to work on a project or something."

"No. That's what I'm trying to tell you. It's nothing like that."

"How can you be sure?"

"Because before I could even get out of the diner and drive home to check on her, someone called me here. It was a man, and he said they've kidnapped Janie."

Her voice broke again but she continued. "He said not to call the police or they'd kill her. Jack, they told me to call you instead."

He shook his head, trying to comprehend what he was hearing. It wasn't adding up.

"Call me? Why would they want you to call me? Edie, you've got to call the police. Hang up and do it right now. Every minute's worth of delay is another mile farther away the kidnappers can be. The police can get out an Amber Alert, they can—"

"NO!" Edie screamed into the phone but got herself back under control before continuing. She was already beginning to grow hoarse from crying. "No, Jack. Haven't you been listening to me? They said they'd kill her if I called the police. They said they'd know if I did it and they would kill her."

"But—"

"They told me to call *you*, Jack. They said I should call you and tell you to check your email, and that you would know what to do."

Silence as Jack tried to absorb her words.

"What does that mean, Jack?"

"I don't know yet." The sick feeling grew inside his stomach. He began to suspect he *did* know, at least in a very general way, and that suspicion did nothing to ease his concern.

He cleared his throat. Edie's breathing sounded heavy and anguished through the telephone receiver but she remained silent, allowing him to work through everything she'd said.

"Can you get someone to watch the diner for you?"

"I'm way ahead of you. There's no way I could continue to work right now. Mark's going to keep an eye on things." Mark was Edie's cook and had been with her since the day the diner opened, right its purchase by after Edie and her husband.

"Okay. Get in your car and come to my house, can you do that?"

"Of course. I'll be there in fifteen minutes." She already sounded considerably more under control now that she had a purpose. It was obvious she viewed driving to Jack's as the first step toward getting her child back, and she was instantly ready to do it.

"Listen to me," Jack said. "I know how upset you are. Be careful driving. Janie's counting on you, and you'll be no good to her if you wrap your car around a tree or a telephone pole."

"I'll be careful," she said. "But I'm not going to waste any time getting there, either."

"I don't blame you," he said, but she had already hung up.

Jack replaced the phone on its cradle, omelet forgotten, dirty dishes forgotten. The sensation of dread crawled through his gut like an advancing army. He walked distractedly into his living room and took a seat in front of his computer.

# 9

Something under the car was squeaking.

Janie wondered what it was, because she'd never heard that kind of noise coming from under Mommy's car before. But it was hard to concentrate because she was really, really tired and her head was pounding and her tummy felt queasy, like the time she'd taken a big gulp of her mommy's soda before realizing it was a grown-up drink, and not a soda at all.

She tried to remember the last time she'd woken up feeling this sick and couldn't do it.

So she kept her eyes closed because the darkness helped make her headache feel a little better. She listened to the oddly comforting sound of the spring or the shock absorber, or whatever metallic thingie was making that squeaking noise under the car, and concentrated on not puking.

She wondered where Mommy was taking her. They were definitely on a highway. The sensation of speed irritated her upset tummy, although the hum of tires on pavement was almost as soothing as the squeaking noise.

She opened her mouth to ask Mommy where they were going when she remembered.

She remembered everything.

She'd been walking home from school with the usual group of kids. One by one her friends had left to go into their houses and eventually the group was whittled down to just Janie and her best friend Samantha Stewart.

Janie said goodbye to Sam, and as she turned toward her house she saw a big blue car idling on the side of the road halfway between the Stewart's driveway and hers. She remembered thinking it was an odd sight. She'd never seen the car before. It didn't belong to anyone in the neighborhood.

And why was it just sitting there on the side of the road?

As she got closer, she remembered thinking maybe she should cross to the other side of the road. The car was making her a little nervous. But before she could do it, the car's door had opened and a man got out and then she would have felt weird crossing the road because the man would have known she was afraid of him and he probably would have felt bad.

So she kept walking and as she did, she became a little less afraid and a little more curious. The man was holding a camera. It wasn't working right, she could tell, because as he held it to his face he was messing around with the lens.

He walked forward, aiming the camera at something behind her as she approached, and for a second she thought they were going to collide because he was concentrating so hard on the stupid camera he didn't even seem to notice she was there. She remembered stepping to the side to go around him.

That was when things got hazy.

She had a vague, milky recollection, kind of a fuzzy black-and-white memory, of a cloth being stuck in her face. The cloth was oily and smelly, worse than just about anything she had ever encountered, and that was where the memories stopped until she woke up a couple of minutes ago with the awful headache.

The squeaking noise was still coming from under the car, but it was no longer soothing or comforting. All Janie could think about was how she'd never heard that noise—or any noise even remotely like it—coming from Mommy's car. And she had ridden in Mommy's car a lot.

That fact, combined with the memory of the man sticking the stinky cloth into her face, made her scared.

What if she wasn't in Mommy's car at all?

What if she was in…that weird camera guy's car?

She still hadn't opened her eyes because her headache continued to pound. But now she wanted to keep her eyes closed for a second reason: maybe if she did so she would fall back to sleep.

And if she fell back to sleep, maybe she would then wake up in her own bed and this would all just be a really bad, really scary dream. Or even if she didn't wake up in her bed, maybe she would awaken in Mommy's car. That would be almost as good.

But she didn't think that was going to happen, mostly because now that she remembered what had happened with the camera guy she knew there was no way in the world she'd ever be able to get back to sleep.

She took a deep breath and blew it out slowly, just like Mommy had taught her to do when she was little and was learning how not to have tantrums when she got upset. Mommy called it "learning how to behave like an adult."

So Janie breathed in and blew out and when she finished she still didn't feel much like an adult. She tried again and the only thing that changed was she felt really dizzy. Her mouth still tasted nasty thanks to the gross cloth the camera guy had stuck in her face, and her throat felt slick and yucky, like she'd drank a glassful of cooking oil or something.

"Mommy?" She spoke softly, in a voice that was almost a whisper.

She wanted her mommy to answer more than she'd ever wanted anything in her life, even more than she had wanted an American Girl doll for Christmas last year, and that was practically all she'd thought about from Thanksgiving until Christmas morning.

She held her breath, half hopeful and half terrified, waiting to see what would happen.

Nothing happened.

Either she was being ignored or she had spoken too softly to be heard. That squeaky spring seemed to be getting louder, but maybe it was just Janie's imagination. Mommy always said she had a great imagination, so that was probably it.

One more deep breath. In and out. She still felt a lot more like a kid than an adult. A scared little kid.

She raised her voice and tried again. "Mommy?"

It sounded shaky and still weak, like it belonged to somebody else.

"Your mommy's not here. She asked me to take care of you for a while." The voice came from right next to her and even though she'd been expecting an answer she jumped. It was definitely *not* Mommy's voice. It sounded exactly like a voice that might belong to a weird camera guy who would stick a yucky cloth in a girl's face.

"Sh-She did?" That didn't sound like something Mommy would do, but would an adult just lie to her face like that? She couldn't imagine it.

"That's right."

"Then what's the secret word?"

A long silence and then the voice said, "Excuse me?"

The man's voice had changed. It was suddenly harder and sounded angry, and Janie didn't know why. She was only doing what Mommy had always told her to do.

But now she was afraid to answer.

After another silence, this time on her end, the man said, "What are you talking about, kid?"

She screwed up her courage and answered. "You know, the secret word. Mommy always told me that if she ever had to send somebody to pick me up that I wasn't expecting, she would tell them a special word to say so I would know it was safe to go with them."

"She always told you that, huh?"

"Yes. So..."

"So what?"

"Um...so what's the word?" Janie knew Mommy would never forget to use the secret word, and there was no way in the world anyone would ever be able to guess it. She had owned a pet hamster for a while named Fluffy. Fluffy had eventually gotten sick and died, but Janie still thought about her every day. Mommy and Janie had agreed "Fluffy" would make the perfect secret word.

The man didn't say "Fluffy."

He didn't say anything.

Then he laughed, and for some reason that was worse than when he'd sounded angry. "Secret word, huh? Your mom's pretty clever, I have to give her that."

"So...what's the word?"

"Jesus Christ kid, enough. I don't know the goddamned secret word, okay? Just shut up and don't give me any trouble or I'll hit you with another dose of gas and then duct tape your mouth closed."

Tear welled in Janie's eyes and she finally opened them, blinking rapidly. The tears rolled down her cheeks as her head resumed pounding like the giant rolling drum she'd seen in last year's Fourth of July parade, exactly as she'd known it would.

She should have kept her eyes closed. The weird camera guy was next to her, driving a car she didn't recognize, and for the first time she realized her hands were tied together behind her back and her ankles had been secured as well. A heavy blanket covered her from just under her chin all the way down to the floor. Anybody who happened to look inside the car's window would see a resting kid, not a girl who'd been kidnapped and taken away from her mommy.

She sniffled and the man looked across the front seat, annoyed.

She was trying to be brave but it was really hard. Her lower lip quivered and her insides felt like jelly and now she was closer to throwing up than ever. It felt just like that time in first grade when she'd been forced to do Show and Tell in front of the whole class and she got so nervous she puked all over Fluffy's cage.

That was a long time ago, way back in first grade. Now she was a third grader, a big kid, and everybody knew big kids didn't hurl just because they were nervous or scared.

"Where's my mommy?" The words came out almost before she even realized she'd spoken them. It was like they exploded out of her, like she couldn't have held them back if she'd tried.

"I told you already." The man seemed really mad again. "Your mommy wants me to watch you for a while. She said she's tired of your act and wants some peace and quiet. So do I, now that I think about it, so shut your mouth like I told you before."

She couldn't stop the tears this time. She knew she should be brave and was trying to be, but the things the man said were scary and mean.

And they were lies.

Janie didn't know where the weird camera guy was taking her but she knew he was lying about her mommy. Mommy told her every day how much she loved her, and she called her My Perfect

Little Girl and said they could face anything provided they did it together. For a long time after Daddy left, Mommy had cried when she said it, but she had still made sure to say it every day, even though it made her sad.

Mommy would be looking for her; Janie knew she would. She had probably already started. And she would find her, too, and when she did the man driving the car would be really sorry. He had obviously never seen Mommy when she was really mad, or else he wouldn't be acting so mean.

Janie knew she couldn't stop crying so she tried to do it quietly. She consoled herself by imagining all the things Mommy would say to the man when she found him. She guessed some of the words would be Bad Words, the grown-up ones Janie wasn't allowed to say.

Mommy tried not to say them either but sometimes she couldn't help herself when she got really mad. Usually Janie didn't like it when Mommy used those words, but she couldn't wait for her to use them on the weird camera guy.

She smiled thinking about it. It was a trembly smile, and she still hadn't quite stopped crying, but as long as she stayed quiet she didn't think the man driving the car would tape her mouth shut like he'd threatened to do.

She didn't want to find out for sure.

The man ignored her for now and kept driving, and that was just fine with Janie.

# 10

Jack's computer was not a new model; in fact, it was ancient by the standards of modern electronics. The machine was at least a decade-and-a-half old, with a massive tower housing the hard drive. The tower was so big he kept it beside his desk. The speakers were large and clunky and the keyboard looked as though it had been trampled by a herd of elephants.

He'd thought for a long time about replacing the system, maybe with a laptop or even a tablet. But although he wouldn't consider himself a technophobe, he didn't much care about the digital revolution, either. He wasn't one to spend valuable time online, and since the nature of his work was dependent upon secrecy, there would be little to gain—and a lot to lose—with an active presence on social media.

The only reason he even had a computer at all was because he needed it to access the encrypted email account The Organization had set up for him when he began working with Mr. Stanton.

This, though, as he sat waiting for the ancient machine to boot up, was one of the rare times he wished he'd upgraded. Edie was even now rushing to meet him. She was understandably upset and would be looking to him for answers, and until he could access the mysterious email she'd referenced from the kidnappers, he would have none to give.

His initial thought when Edie said Janie had been kidnapped was that her father had taken her. The vast majority of child abductions were directly related to custody issues between estranged parents, so that scenario would seem to make the most sense.

But he'd discarded that theory even before Edie mentioned the email. She'd made it abundantly clear to him over the course of numerous conversations that her greatest regret in life was her husband's willingness to abandon his only child in order to move cross-country with a woman barely out of her teens.

"I could deal with him leaving me," she'd said, her agony painfully clear, "but how could he run out on his own little girl?"

It seemed unlikely in the extreme that a man capable of what Edie's ex had done would suddenly materialize out of nowhere, take Janie and then vanish again.

The fact that the email had been addressed to him made it abundantly clear that *he* was the reason little Janie Tolliver had been taken.

The sick feeling in his stomach clinched it. A man operating on the fringes of society—as Jack had been doing since his military days—learned to trust his instincts, and Jack's were screaming that he was being targeted by Janie's abduction.

The computer clicked and hummed and taunted him with the singular deliberateness with which it approached its mission. After what felt like half an hour but was probably only two or three minutes, its startup applications had launched and Jack hurriedly opened his web browser.

He navigated to his "normal" email account, the one through which he communicated electronically with everyone except The Organization. This would be the account the kidnappers would have had access to.

Finding the specific message was easy, even buried as it was among dozens of spam emails and routine correspondence. It stuck out like a sore thumb the moment Jack's mailbox opened. It was the only one with a subject line reading, FUCK UP AND SHE DIES.

He closed his eyes.

Muttered, "Oh, Christ."

Opened his eyes and then the email, and began reading.

*We assume we now have your full attention*, the message read. *Please allow us to clarify something immediately, since a thorough understanding of the situation is critical to ensuring that everyone involved stays alive and healthy.*

*Thus, be warned: we are in charge, and you are not.*

*We recognize that such a scenario must irk a man of your...unique abilities, shall we say. But that is the situation, and that is how the situation will remain. We strongly suggest you come to grips quickly with this reality and accept the division of power in our relationship. Lives depend on it.*

*The little girl is fine for now, but she will remain so only as long as you do exactly as you are told. Deviate from your instructions in any way—even a minor way—and the lovely Ms. Tolliver will never see her child again. We are not men of patience, Mr. Sheridan, so do not underestimate our resolve unless you wish to explain to a grieving mother how you were responsible for her daughter's death.*

*Having said that, please understand we are not unreasonable men. There is a way you can accomplish the return of Janie Tolliver to her mother's loving arms. There is only one way, but it is eminently doable for a man of your...unique abilities.*

*And the way you can accomplish Janie's return is this: you will assassinate Maryland Governor Jim Studds.*

*You will complete your assignment within seven days of the time and date stamped on this email.*

*You will make the governor's death appear accidental.*

*Simple for a man of your...unique abilities, yes?*

*Be aware, Mr. Sheridan, that none of these conditions are negotiable. If you elect not to complete your assignment, or if you elect to inform the authorities of our arrangement, or if you take any action we deem suspicious or not in keeping with your assignment—and we will know—little Janie will die, and in the most, shall we say, DISAGREEABLE manner imaginable.*

*It will not be pretty.*

*We told you earlier we are not unreasonable men. We will prove as much in a show of good faith soon. Stay by your telephone. We will call within the hour and allow Ms. Tolliver to speak to her child to establish proof of life.*

*But do not misinterpret our gesture of good faith as weakness. Make that mistake and neither you nor Ms. Tolliver will ever see her daughter or hear from us again.*

The email was of course unsigned, and as he finished reading Jack realized he'd been holding his breath. He expelled it in an explosive burst punctuated with a curse. His worst fears had just been realized, and almost immediately after beginning his first real relationship in decades. He'd spent most of his adult life living a solitary existence out of a desire to avoid any possibility of placing a loved one in harm's way, and now a defenseless child was in grave danger and her mother's world had been shattered.

And it was all because of him.

He read through the email again, not sure what he was looking for other than some indication of its author's identity. The sentence structure and phrasing suggested a level of education beyond what one would normally expect out of someone capable of kidnapping a child in order to coerce a man to commit murder.

Of course, any group committed to assassinating a sitting governor was probably far removed from the typical kidnapping-for-ransom scenario. And although Jack's career had brought him in contact with plenty of people capable such a despicable act, none came immediately to mind as a suspect. Most of the people he'd encountered who possessed the sociopathic tendencies necessary to become involved in such a plot were no longer walking the earth.

The kidnapper could be someone he knew or it could be someone with whom he was completely unfamiliar.

He'd just begun examining the email for the third time when his front door opened and Edie Tolliver burst through it like a running back hitting the line in an NFL game.

He looked up and his heart broke. Edie wasn't one to spend hours in front of a mirror putting herself together; she possessed a natural beauty that rendered any such effort unnecessary. But the distressed female standing in front of him barely resembled the beautiful young woman he'd come to know and begun to fall in love with.

Her jacket hung haphazardly off her petite frame, the buttons and buttonholes unmatched.

Her blonde hair, normally framing her face in a sexy shag, looked as though it had been styled in a wind tunnel.

Her face was drawn and lined with tension and for the first time since Jack had met her, she looked every bit her thirty-something years of age. She was trying to hold herself together but was losing the battle.

She ran toward him and he barely had time to rise from his chair before she crashed into him like a guided missile. She nearly knocked him off his feet but he wrapped his arms around her and held her tightly, her entire body shivering like a bird with a broken wing.

The moment she felt his touch she began to sob.

"My baby's gone," she said in a whisper. "Why would someone take my baby?"

He'd never felt as ineffectual as he did right now.

He rubbed her arms, wishing he could warm her up, knowing the chill she was experiencing was unrelated to the temperature inside his house. After a moment he led her to a comfortable stuffed chair—the only truly plush chair he owned—and eased her into it. He knelt on the carpeted floor and took her hand gently.

Edie looked into Jack's face through bloodshot eyes brimming with tears. When she spoke, her voice was surprisingly clear, considering the situation. "Who would do something like this, Jack? And why would they involve you? What the hell is going on?"

He wanted to avert his eyes. Wanted to look anywhere but into this woman's tortured gaze. The last thing he wanted was to hurt her, but that ship had sailed with Janie's disappearance.

Now he owed her the truth, and although it would undoubtedly result in the end of their relationship and the justifiable hatred of him from the woman he loved, he would make good on that debt.

Jack cleared his throat. It felt hot. Parched.

"I'm not who you think I am," he said.

# 11

Edie shook her head. "What does that mean? And what does it have to do with Janie? Can't it wait?"

"I'm afraid it has everything to do with Janie. It's why she was kidnapped."

"I don't understand."

"I'm not some sort of traveling businessman, as least not in the sense you think I am. I examined the kidnappers' email while you were on your way over here, and it verified my suspicions. Janie was not a random victim. She was specifically targeted by a man or a group, and for a specific purpose."

"What kind of purpose?"

"To be used as leverage against me."

"I'm not following you. Leverage for what? And how is sitting here having this conversation helping get my baby back? You said yourself that with every minute that goes by she could be a mile farther away."

Jack released her hand. He stood and met her gaze. It was terrified and hopeful and confused and impatient.

It was heartbreaking.

And this was all his fault.

He cleared his throat. "I know you want to get right to work finding Janie and getting her back. That's what I want, too, and I promise that's exactly what's going to happen. But the things I'm telling you now are critical. They're things you need to know, things that will directly impact our recovery of Janie."

Edie stared wordlessly.

"They're things I should have told you before now."

"Then get on with it."

Jack breathed deeply and plunged ahead. "You already know I was in the military."

"Of course. You served in Iraq and Afghanistan."

"Among other places, yes."

"So? What does that have to do with anything?"

"I never told you specifically what my mission was in the Middle East."

Edie shrugged. "And that never bothered me. I just assumed you didn't want to talk about the things you'd seen over there."

"And you're right about that, as far as it goes. But it's not just things I saw that I didn't want to talk about, it's things I did."

Distracting Edie's restless mind from dwelling on what might be happening to her little girl seemed to have strengthened her, at least a bit. Her voice sounded more like itself and she seemed to have stopped shaking. More or less.

When she spoke, her tone was gentle. "Jack, I'm sure you did things you're not proud of during your military service. But you served in wartime, and during a non-traditional war at that. My dad told me once that a soldier's job is to kill people and break things, and while I can't automatically condone war—certainly not all wars—I'm also not about to fault you for doing your job as a soldier."

God, he admired this woman. He was falling more in love with her, which made what would inevitably follow this discussion much more difficult. But it was too late to stop now, and more to the point, Edie deserved a full accounting of his failings.

He owed it to her.

He tore his eyes from hers and fixed them on the floor. "I haven't told you everything yet."

For the first time, he was ashamed of himself and the direction his life had taken after leaving the armed forces. "I haven't come close to telling you everything."

"So tell me now."

"When I was in the desert, I learned a lot about myself and about human nature. I discovered there are people in this world so evil, so destructive, so dangerous, so black-hearted, that eventually they forfeit their right to life. I discovered I have a peculiar talent, one that's exceedingly rare."

Edie spread her hands. "Go on."

"I have a talent for eliminating those evil people. In fact, it was my primary mission while I was overseas."

"I already told you," Edie said, still speaking softly. "I understand war is brutal. I understand people do things on the battlefield that they would never consider doing in the civilian world. I don't blame you for your actions in the Middle East, Jack."

"It wasn't just in the Middle East, and it wasn't just during my time in the service. That's what I'm trying to tell you. Since leaving the army, I've made a career out of doing the same thing here in the states. It's my talent. It's what I know. It's the *only* thing I know. I eliminate evil people."

Jack stared steadfastly at the floor, unable to meet her eyes as silence filled the room and then lengthened. The silence stretched on for so long that he began to think maybe she hadn't understood what he said. It wasn't like the words were anything she'd ever expected to hear.

When he could no longer stand the tension, he steeled himself and raised his eyes. Edie had never looked so small or so fragile. She seemed to have shrunk into the chair and she stared back at him with wide, frightened eyes.

He knelt beside the chair and tried to take her hand but she pulled it away.

"And that's why my baby is gone? Someone took her because of your...*career?*" The venom she put into the last word formed a jarring counterpoint to the dull monotone of the rest of the sentence. Her eyes had glazed over and she sat motionless in the big stuffed chair.

Jack wondered if she might be going into shock. Between learning her daughter had been kidnapped and then discovering the man she thought she knew was actually a killer, it would certainly be understandable.

He nodded. "Yes."

He wanted her to scream at him, to leap to her feet and pummel him, to grab a lamp off the end table and swing the heavy base at his skull. He wouldn't stop her if she did. He deserved all that and more.

But she didn't scream and she didn't jump to her feet and she didn't hit him. She sat in the chair, seeming to grow smaller and more insubstantial by the second, and she stared at him dully as if looking at a stranger.

Someone to be feared.

He supposed he was.

She shifted her gaze, her eyes meandering around a room she had seen dozens of times. When they stopped, she gazed steadfastly at something—or nothing—over Jack's left shoulder, refusing to look at him. He began to think she might sit lifeless and unmoving in his living room chair forever.

Then she spoke. The words came out in the same monotone she'd used before, slowly and without inflection.

But she spoke. "You said you're good at what you do. Is that true, or is that a lie, too?"

Jack hadn't thought his shame could get any more complete or his heart could break any further, but he was wrong. Her words were like a blade slicing through his ribs. But still they were no more than he deserved.

He took a moment to answer, unwilling to speak for fear of breaking down. Then he swallowed heavily and said, "Yes. I'm very good at what I do. It's what I was trained for."

He dropped his eyes again. "It's who I am."

"Can you get my baby back?"

"Yes, I can get Janie back. But it won't be easy and I'll need your help. Can you focus for me and do your part?"

Anger flashed in Edie's pretty eyes. The slack expression disappeared in an instant and she glared at him incredulously. "Can I do *my* part to get my little girl back? Can I focus on helping you when it's *your* fault she's gone? How dare you ask me that? How *dare* you? "

Jack pursed his lips, stung by her words but relieved to see some of her spark return. Quiet acquiescence was not Edie Tolliver. She was a fighter through and through, and she would need every bit of that fighting spirit to get through what was coming.

She had nearly been screaming, and now she lowered her voice.

The tears brimming in her eyes finally spilled over and ran down her cheeks. "I'll do whatever it takes to get Janie back, don't you *ever* doubt that."

"Okay," he said, letting his rational, operative brain take command.

When this was all over, and he'd gotten Janie back from whoever had taken her, he had some serious thinking to do, some real reassessment of his life and priorities. Obviously it would be too late to salvage any kind of relationship with Edie, but reflection would still be necessary. In fact, it was long overdue. His life would have to change, even without Edie and Janie in it.

But for now, introspection would have to take a back seat to action, and the pain would have to be sealed away and compartmentalized. The life of an innocent seven-year-old depended on it.

"Okay," he repeated. "The first thing you need to understand is that Janie is unharmed. I promise you that."

"You can't make that kind of promise. You have no way of knowing whether she's safe." Her voice was cold.

"She's safe, Edie. She was taken for a reason, and that reason was to establish control over me. To get me to do something the kidnappers know I would not otherwise do."

"To kill someone."

Deep breath.

"Yes. To kill someone. But the point is until I complete the task they've set for me, Janie is a valuable commodity. She's the only leverage they have, and it's to their benefit to keep her safe and out of harm's way. There is no sexual component to this kidnapping—" Edie winced and sobbed and Jack pressed on—"and there is no revenge component, where the perpetrators want to get back at me by hurting someone I care about."

"You've done that perfectly well on your own."

"Yes, I have. I know that and I'll never forgive myself for it. But until I get Janie home safely my only concern is going to be what is best for her, and I know it will be yours as well."

"Of course it will. I already told you that."

Jack nodded. "Then take what I'm telling you to heart. Janie's safe, and will remain so until I get to her."

Edie ran a hand over her face, which was normally bright and pretty and smiling but this afternoon looked haggard and worn. Ancient.

"But she's so little," she whispered. "And she doesn't know where she is or who she's with. She's just so little," she repeated.

"She's little but she's tough, just like her mom. She'll be strong and she'll get through this. You have to be strong, too, because she's going to need you when she gets home."

No response.

"You're both going to be okay, Edie."

She choked out a bitter laugh that was half-sob. "I guess your definition of 'okay' must be different than mine. My little girl's gone, taken hostage to be used as 'leverage' to force my new boyfriend, who by the way happens to be a contract killer, to murder an undoubtedly innocent person. Just what in holy hell is 'okay' about any of that?"

Her voice had started to shake and crack again, and Jack feared she might descend back into the near-comatose state she'd previously exhibited. But she lifted her chin when she finished speaking and glared at Jack defiantly.

He remained silent. What was there to say?

"So are you going to do it?" she whispered. "Are you going to murder someone to get Janie back?"

Jack shook his head firmly. "Killing the person they want dead wouldn't get Janie back. All it would do is seal her fate. Remember I told you I know Janie's safe because she's their only leverage over me?"

Edie nodded, her eyes now glued to Jack's. They were wide and terrified, but they'd finally gotten into subject matter she cared about. Her child.

"Well," he continued, "The minute I complete the task they've set for me, Janie becomes a liability. Presumably she's seen their faces, but even if not, they won't want to take the chance that she has, or that she can identify them by voice or in some other way. If I kill the person they've instructed me to, we'll never see Janie alive again."

Edie had closed her eyes as Jack spoke and now she moaned softly. The sound was one of utter, abject agony and it carved his broken heart up into tiny slivers.

"I'm telling you this because you need to know the truth," he said. "Don't misunderstand me. I can and will get Janie back, but it won't be by doing the bidding of these ruthless slimeballs."

Silence fell over the darkening room again; both occupants lost in their own private pain.

Finally Edie spoke. "Let's get started, then. What do we do first?"

# 12

Mike Hargus brought the car to a stop in front of a single-story white clapboard cottage. A trail of dust swirled around the car and began to settle, the product of a dirt driveway and an unseasonably dry stretch of weather.

The cottage had been in Mike's family for decades and was one of the few things he'd managed to retain in the divorce, which had taken place years ago but which still irked him to no end. Half his savings, gone. Half his investments, gone. Half of every goddamned thing gone with the stroke of a pen on a divorce agreement.

He'd worked hard to build up the now-badly-depleted nest egg, doing legal as well as illegal chores for Bradley Chilcott that would turn the stomach of any ordinary man, while his bitch of a wife had sat around on her admittedly sexy ass, criticizing and critiquing until Mike just couldn't stand it any more.

That was what he told himself.

Somewhere deep down inside, though, in the lonely predawn half-light following another of thousands of sleepless nights, Mike had to admit—if only to himself—that *Lauren* had left *him*, not the other way around. And on her way out the door she'd thrown around words like "controlling," "brutal," "paranoid," and even "psychotic."

Bitch.

The passage of time had led Mike to the conclusion that even after suffering the financial hit, as hard as it was to take, on balance he was better off with the blood-sucking leach out of his life. Fuck her if she couldn't see how good she'd had it with him.

And he *had* been permitted to keep his family's cottage in the settlement. Technically, half the cottage belonged to Mike's brother, but Mike couldn't remember the last time Jimmy had driven all the way up here.

The place was no great prize, having settled into a kind of semi-ramshackle decay after years of neglect. The siding was weathered and badly in need of a fresh coat of paint, roofing shingles fell like giant grey snowflakes in a high wind, and a series of loose floorboards on the back deck made navigating it an iffy proposition.

Mike's lack of maintenance was probably what had kept the cottage in his family. Lauren had always hated it, and even in the early years of their marriage, when she'd still at least pretended to like him, she had visited just once and then steadfastly refused to return.

Bitch.

But the cottage was still livable, more or less, and the perfect place in which to stash his prize for a week or so. Located on the north side of New Hampshire's Lake Winnipesaukee, on a lot carved out of extreme wilderness, the place was isolated and remote. Despite Winnipesaukee's status as a New England tourist attraction, the lake's one hundred eighty miles of shoreline—much of it rocky and forbidding—meant privacy was assured. An occupant of Mike's cottage could reasonably expect to go days without seeing another human being besides the occasional water-skier far out on the lake.

Mike typically spent a week or so up here in the summer when he could get the time off from that slave-driver Chilcott, and by the end of the vacation was inevitably itching to get away from Mother Nature and back to the land of cars and liquor, fast food and faster women.

If he was being honest with himself, the extreme isolation kind of gave him the willies. But this week's duty shouldn't be too bad. His only responsibility would be to watch over one hostage, and a little kid at that.

And he would have company. The snot-nosed little brat was so important that Chilcott had given Mike permission to recruit one of his acquaintances, a drug dealer/B-and-E man named Byron Hunt, to babysit with him. They would offer Hunt five grand and in exchange he would help keep watch over the kid, allowing them twenty-four hours a day of direct supervision without having to miss a minute of sleep.

Once the job was complete, Hunt would find himself at the bottom of a shallow grave in the almost unlimited expanse of wilderness surrounding the cottage, and the five grand would find its way into Mike's pocket, and no one would ever be the wiser.

Mike shook his head. He'd been lost in his thoughts and had absolutely no idea how long he and the little girl had been parked outside the cottage sitting like idiots inside his stolen car.

That sort of thing had been happening more and more, where he'd zone out and lose minutes or even hours of time, and while there was no question the situation was scary as hell, now was not the time to worry about it. All he had to do was keep his shit together for a week and the Chilcott gravy train would be back on the tracks.

And once that train was rolling again and moving toward the White House, the real money would start pouring in. Bribes and kickbacks and graft, a pile of riches Bradley Chilcott would be forced to share with his top security man, if for no other reason than Mike Hargus knew where the bodies were buried.

Literally, in some cases.

And that mountain of cash would make the measly hundred grand Lauren had taken in the divorce look like the contents of a kid's piggy bank. *Like the contents of little Janie Tolliver's piggy bank,* Mike thought and snickered.

Then he blinked several times and jumped in his seat.

Christ, he'd zoned out again. *Keep it together, you asshole.*

He turned toward his captive and saw the Tolliver girl eyeing him curiously. She'd fallen asleep at least an hour ago during the drive to Winnipesauke and the nap must have calmed her nerves, because there was no trace of the teary-eyed, "poor me" attitude she'd exhibited earlier.

"What do you think you're looking at?" he said gruffly. He was pissed off and embarrassed she'd witnessed his behavior but didn't know why. She was a fucking seven-year-old; who gave a damn what she thought? It wasn't like she was going to live to tell anyone she'd seen her kidnapper acting like a mental patient.

"I'm not crying," she said defiantly, as if announcing a major victory. Given her age and situation, Mike supposed it was.

"Good," he replied. "Make sure you don't start. All that will happen is you'll make me mad, and that's not something you want to experience."

"I have to pee," she said as if he'd never spoken.

"Jesus Christ," he grumbled to himself. "Why did it have to be a kid?"

"What?"

"Nothing. Just hold it a little longer. We'll be in the house in a minute and you can go in there, okay?" Mike sprang out of the car and hurried around to the passenger side. The stolen car was no prize—several years old and as anonymous a sedan as you were likely to find on the road—but it was all the wheels he was going to have for the next week and the prospect of driving to the liquor store in a car stinking of piss held no appeal whatsoever.

He glanced quickly in all directions to reassure himself the area was deserted—*of course it's deserted; it's always deserted around here*—and then opened the passenger door. He threw the blanket off the kid and fumbled for the handcuff keys. Bent and uncuffed her ankles.

Then he stood and yanked her out of the car by the elbow. She let out a little squeak of surprise and cringed.

"Now you listen to me," he said sternly, pointing to the cottage. "You're going to walk straight into that house. You're not going to run and you're not going to scream and you're not going to give me any kind of trouble, because if you do it will just make me mad, and that's—"

"I know," she said, interrupting him mid-rant. "That's something I don't want to experience."

Mike's initial reaction was to smack her. He hated being interrupted, especially by a smart-mouthed little bitch who didn't even have the common sense to be frightened. Without thinking he lifted his right arm to backhand the brat right across the face. Then he remembered the importance of keeping the girl unharmed—for now—and stopped himself. He settled for growl-ing, "Don't be a wiseass, kid, it's a good way to get hurt."

"You shouldn't use bad language," she said, meeting his gaze straight on. "Mommy says it makes you look ignorant."

"Oh, Mommy says that, does she?"

"Yup." The girl stood on tiptoes to peer curiously at the house over Mike's shoulder. Her knees jiggled unconsciously. "Can we go inside now? I guess you forgot but I still have to pee."

*I'm going to enjoy pulling the trigger on you,* he thought. *Maybe this week isn't going to be quite as relaxed as I'd hoped.* He grabbed the girl by the shoulder and shoved her in the direction of the front door.

"Ignorant, my ass," he mumbled. He turned and followed his captive up the steps, grumbling all the way.

# 13

Jack sat in front of his computer waiting impatiently for a program to load. The software was called *Mole* and it was highly classified. It was so secret, in fact, that as a civilian, Jack should not even have been aware of its existence, never mind having it installed on his computer.

But he *was* aware.

And it *was* installed.

Years ago, while working in the Middle East, Jack had saved the life of a fellow operator named Bill Earl during a mission gone sideways. The pair had been tasked with eliminating am Afghani crime lord, a bloodthirsty man responsible for decades of child sex slavery, drug manufacturing and murder.

The plan had been simple: break into the crime lord's home while he was sleeping and put two silenced 9mm slugs into his skull. Unlike many of Jack's missions, this one carried no requirement that the man's death appear accidental or natural.

The only reason the army had even become aware of this particular tribal leader was through a confidential Afghani source whose family lived in the area, and the mission's only purpose was to eliminate the iron-fisted grip the crime lord had maintained over his village.

But they'd been fed faulty intel, and instead of entering the Afghani's bedroom when they infiltrated the house they had found themselves inside the room of the man's teenage daughter. She'd woken up and begun screaming, and rather than killing her, the pair had elected to spare her, to backtrack and fight their way out of the house through the man's now-awake and alert security team.

Bill Earl had taken a bullet to the chest. The slug punctured a lung and fractured two ribs, and extreme blood loss rendered him unconscious within minutes. Jack refused to even consider leaving him. He'd dragged the bleeding, badly injured man through the house with his left hand while holding off the security team with the weapon in his right. He'd been certain he was going to die and even now, years later, wasn't entirely sure how he survived.

After putting down all three members of the Afghani's security team, Jack had staggered eight miles to his unit's secure location with Bill Earl slung over his shoulder in a fireman's carry, all while dodging an intense manhunt initiated by the still-breathing—and now severely pissed-off—Afghani.

Six weeks later Jack returned to the house, alone, and completed the mission.

To say Bill Earl's family had been grateful would be an understatement. The mission had been classified, of course, so most of the relevant details he could never share with them. But they knew Jack had saved his partner through extraordinary effort and at extreme risk to himself.

He'd earned an entire family of loyal friends for life.

That family included a brother, Ron Earl, a computer genius and technology expert who earned a living writing computer code and software programs for the NSA.

When Jack met Ron following Bill Earl's return home for life-saving surgery, the two hit it off immediately, and Ron had made him a promise: "Anything you need, anytime or anywhere, you let me know and if it's in my power to give, you'll have it. No questions asked."

Jack shrugged off the offer, humbled by the man's sincerity but unsure what a computer expert would ever have to offer someone like him, to whom just signing into his email account was an adventure.

But that was before Jack's entry into The Organization, and the civilian continuation of a career he'd begun when barely out of his teens and in service to the United States government.

And also before he began hearing rumors through his many contacts still active in the intelligence community of a super-secret computer program in development. A program so sophisticated it was capable of breaking through virtually any known electronic firewall and then tracking the movement of any piece of electronic data.

The significance to the government of this kind of software—if it actually existed—was obvious. It would allow the United States to monitor terrorist activity and track the movement of weapons, troops and dangerous materials of entities hostile to the U.S. to a degree never before possible.

The significance to someone like Jack Sheridan of this kind of software—if it actually existed—was equally obvious. It would allow him the potential to identify entities hostile to *him* in the event he or someone he cared about were to be targeted for blackmail or other mischief.

Exactly as had happened today.

Jack had given plenty of thought to the implications of acquiring such a program—if it even existed—before ever making a move. Were he to be apprehended with it loaded onto his computer's hard drive he would certainly be jailed, maybe even charged with treason. There was no legitimate reason for any ordinary citizen to possess *Mole* and as far as anyone knew, Jack was just an ordinary citizen.

And his fervent hope was that he would never need it or anything like it. He was cautious to a fault, and religiously observant of his personal rule never to get close to anyone who could become a target.

But things had a way of going south in a hurry in his career field, and even the most cautious operators eventually make mistakes. So Jack had very discreetly contacted Ron Earl. After a delicate dance conducted over the course of several weeks, he'd verified that *Mole* did in fact exist, and that not only was the program real, Ron Earl himself had been one of its primary developers.

Jack never even had to remind Ron of his years-earlier promise. He made a generous monetary offer to purchase a copy of the *Mole* program, and that offer was accepted without hesitation or negotiation.

Ron knew Jack was still involved in some way in the field of covert ops, and Jack's selfless actions in Afghanistan—when he could have abandoned Bill Earl to a horrific fate and no one would ever have known—were enough to convince Ron there was no risk to the transaction.

Weeks later Jack had become the somewhat reluctant owner of one of the most powerful espionage/intelligence tools ever developed. He'd loaded *Mole* onto his computer—itself disguised and hidden under several layers of encryption designed to render it invisible to anyone but the program's owner—and forgotten about it. He'd had no need for it so he'd never used it.

Until now.

The program loaded sluggishly and for a moment Jack feared his aging computer would not be powerful enough to run it. The delay was made more difficult by Edie's presence in the chair across the room, her fear and desperation—and cold revulsion for Jack—making itself plain despite her lack of complaint.

At last a muted *ding* indicated *Mole* had finished booting up and was ready for use. Jack wracked his brain trying to recall the instructions Ron Earl had given him regarding use of the program. He *did* remember Ron telling him the developers had constructed *Mole* to be as user-friendly as possible, with the understanding that the intelligence specialists who would be utilizing the program would in most cases not be computer experts.

He began slowly, afraid of making a mistake that might shut down the program and force him to start over. As he worked he realized Edie had climbed out of his stuffed chair and was standing directly behind him, watching closely. He couldn't see her but he didn't have to. Simmering anger and frosty disapproval surrounded her like a force field.

And he didn't blame her a bit. She had every right to hate him.

After a few minutes—and more than a few mistakes—Jack decided he was ready to load the email he'd received into *Mole*.

He had not a single doubt that the communication had been routed through numerous secure servers designed to render it untraceable and ensure its originator remained anonymous. And in practically every case, that routing would have been successful.

But this wasn't every case. Jack had *Mole* on his side and he was certain whoever had written and sent the email was unaware of the program's existence.

He liked his chances of tracing it.

He also had no idea how long it would take *Mole* to do its job.

Maybe it would be nearly instantaneous.

Maybe not.

He waited in front of the computer screen as the program—hopefully—performed its magic. There was no way to know whether anything at all was happening, aside from some random-sounding clicking and whirring coming from deep inside Jack's computer.

After a few minutes with no results he decided his hopes for a quick resolution had been misguided. He stood and stretched and turned to see Edie Tolliver still watching him from behind hooded eyes.

He averted his gaze and walked into the kitchen to make tea. All his hopes were resting on Ron Earl's creation. If *Mole* didn't perform as advertised, Jack had no idea what he was going to do next.

It wasn't a comforting feeling.

When the tea had steeped, Jack picked up the two mugs and returned to the living room to wait. He handed one to Edie. She accepted it without comment and then turned and padded back to her chair.

He wondered if she would ever speak to him again.

He doubted it.

There didn't seem to be anything left to say.

# 14

The girl was secured.

The wise-ass attitude she'd displayed when they arrived at the cottage disappeared when Mike chained her to an old, rusted radiator, and he felt a momentary rush of savage pleasure at putting the little bitch back in her place.

But it was only momentary. He immediately wished for the previous incarnation of Janie Tolliver when she began crying again and asking—constantly—for her mommy. She seemed ready to launch into a fit of screaming hysterics but Mike put a stop to that shit by calmly informing her that if she uttered one single sound above the decibel level of a normal speaking voice she would be gagged and hog-tied to the foldup cot he'd provided her to sleep on for the next week.

He wasn't sure she understood what it meant to be hog-tied, but she seemed to have no problem comprehending the concept of the gag. The threat effectively staved off any hysterics, and when he left the room to walk into the cottage's combination living/dining area the kid was sniffling into her pillow and refusing to look at him.

Good.

The hard part of the plan—at least from Mike's perspective—had been kidnapping Janie Tolliver in broad daylight from almost directly in front of her house and getting away cleanly. With that accomplished, the remainder—again, from Mike's perspective—should be a breeze.

Byron Hunt would be arriving in a couple of hours to keep him company and help watch the captive, and while Sheridan was off doing the heavy lifting of assassinating Maryland Governor Jim Studds, Mike and Byron would be several hundred miles away playing whist, smoking cigars and monitoring news reports to find out when Studds bit the dust.

Mike had agreed to call Bradley Chilcott the moment Phase One of their plan—kidnapping and stashing the little girl—was complete. He supposed he should do that now, although he was strongly tempted to wait a while before checking in, just to fuck with the controlling bastard.

Maybe he'd celebrate completing Phase One with a gin and tonic or a beer before making the call.

He mulled it over. Went back and forth on the matter. Chilcott wasn't a bad guy, he supposed, for a power-hungry megalomaniac, but something about the prissy asshole's sense of superiority went right up Mike's ass. Sideways.

Therefore, Mike enjoyed tweaking his boss whenever he could. Not enough to risk getting fired and losing his spot on the Chilcott Presidential Gravy Train, but enough to let the guy know that Mike wasn't intimidated by a soft politician who'd probably never been in a fistfight since the last time his little sister beat him up in the backyard.

Finally he sighed and picked up his cell phone. Might as well get the damned call over with. He wasn't going to be able to truly relax until he'd hung up with Chilcott. That, more than anything else, ended up being the deciding factor.

He punched the lieutenant governor's speed dial number and waited, growing increasingly annoyed listening to the electronic buzzing that indicated the phone was ringing—but not being picked up—on the other end.

Chilcott was fucking with *him*. He must be. There was no possible way the son of a bitch was doing anything other than waiting nervously by the phone for Mike to call. They'd gone over the plan dozens of times, so Chilcott was every bit as aware as Mike of the plan's timing.

From the arrival of the kids in Tolliver's neighborhood, to the distance from that neighborhood to Mike's cottage on the shores of Lake Winnipesaukee, everything had been meticulously plotted and timed out, right down to the minute.

Mike had explained that there would be some slippage, that things in the field never went as smoothly as the operator expected them to, that the actual execution of Phase One would almost certainly take longer than expected. But even assuming Chilcott had understood Mike's point, it was simply inconceivable to think the lieutenant governor was reviewing some stupid budget item, or doing *anything* other than sitting at his desk sweating his ass off awaiting Mike's call.

The phone rang several times and he knew it was about to go to voice mail. He couldn't remember how many rings it took for that to happen, but he'd called Chilcott so damned many times over the course of his employment he could sense exactly when it was going to happen.

If Chilcott didn't pick up by the time the voice mail message came on Mike would hang up. He certainly wasn't going to leave evidence of an incriminating nature in a goddamned electronic mailbox.

And if he had to hang up, he would wait hours before trying again. Hours. Let the boss stew in his own juices for a good long while. Maybe he'd even wait until tomorrow to call. And he certainly wouldn't answer Chilcott's calls. He would let the son-of-a-bitch become more and more frantic, string him along, make him wait until—

"Hello?"

Finally. Mike had begun pulling the phone away from his ear by the time Chilcott answered. The boss was trying to play it cool but Mike could hear the tension in his voice.

"Yeah," he said after a satisfying delay. "It's me. Took you long enough to pick up. Busy meeting with the guy you're going to replace in the statehouse?"

"Don't be a wiseass. Is Phase One complete?"

"Of course. Did you expect anything else?"

"You were the one who said anything and everything can happen in the field."

"Yeah, well, regardless, everything went fine. The package is nice and secure inside the post office. There were no problems with delivery."

"So we're ready to move on to Phase Two?"

"Ready as we'll ever be."

"Okay. Make the call. Then get back to me. I want to be kept apprised."

"Will do." Mike hung up and shook his head. *I want to be kept apprised.* Who the hell talked like that?

# 15

Jack and Edie had been sitting silently, avoiding looking at each other, for who knew how long. At least half an hour.

Finally Jack cleared his throat and spoke. "We need to discuss the phone call we're going to get."

"What about it? All I care about is talking to Janie. I need to know she's alive and okay."

"I understand, but we have to play this the right way."

"*Play it the right way?* This is no game. Those monsters have my baby."

"Edie, listen to me. I apologize for the poor choice of words, but it's important we approach this properly."

"What do you mean?"

"We have to make clear to them that they need us—or me, at least—just as much as we need them. They feel they're dealing from a position of power, and I acknowledge that they are. But until I do what they want, I hold some, too."

He could tell his point was lost on the distraught woman, and he couldn't really blame her. The only thing in the world that mattered to her was the opportunity to talk to her missing child.

He stopped talking and they resumed their silent vigil.

\* \* \*

When the phone rang they both jumped.

Even though the email had told them specifically to expect a call, even though they had been waiting on pins and needles *for* that call, the sound of the ringer jangling through Jack's much-too-silent home felt rude, an unwelcome intrusion, a dirty joke whispered in church.

They leapt to their feet simultaneously. Edie reached for the phone but Jack grabbed hold of her upper arm.

"Let it ring a couple of times," he said. He stared into her eyes, captivated as always by their radiant blue.

"Let it ring? Why? That's my little girl on the line!"

"I know. But we already talked about this. We have to establish some kind of control."

She grunted unhappily and as the phone rang a second time Jack said, "Tell me again what you're going to do."

"Stay calm. Let them know you'll follow their instructions to the letter. Insist on talking to Janie every day." She ticked the items off on her fingers impatiently and then reached again for the phone.

This time Jack let her answer. He wasn't sure he could have stopped her again anyway.

She took a deep breath. "Hello?" She held the receiver tilted away from her ear so Jack could hear.

"Mommy?" The voice sounded small and forlorn and tears began to roll down Edie's cheeks as she struggled to hold herself together.

"Yes baby, it's Mommy. I'm right here, honey."

"I want to come home. When can I come home?"

"Very soon, baby, I promise. Are you okay? Has anyone hurt you?"

"Mommy, what's going on? Why can't I—"

Janie's voice faded away as a gravelly-voiced man in the background said, "Alright, enough lovey-dovey bullshit. Gimme the phone."

*It's probably just as well Janie's off the line,* Jack thought. *Edie's losing it. A seven-year-old doesn't need to hear her mom's breakdown.*

Edie clapped a hand to her mouth and began sobbing uncontrollably as the tears fell full-force. One thing this horror show had already taught Jack was that the heart didn't just break and then start healing. That would have been hard enough to handle. Instead, it continued to fracture, over and over, until you began to suspect the pain would never end.

"Okay," Gravel Voice said gruffly. "There you have it. Proof of life. The little brat's fine. For now. Do exactly as you're told, exactly *when* you're told, and she'll stay that way. If you don't, well, let's just say I hope you have a lot of great pictures of her because I promise you will never see her again alive."

Edie's legs gave out and she slid down to the floor with her back against the wall. "Don't hurt her," she pleaded. "She's just a little girl and she's never done anything to anyone."

"Well now, that's out of my hands, isn't it? Whether she lives or dies is entirely up to your boyfriend."

"Jack knows you mean business. He understands that. He recognizes that you're in charge and he's already planning out the job you've asked him to do." Her words came out in a breathy rush, as Edie tried to protect her daughter the only way she could.

"Then you have nothing to worry about, do you? Now put Mr. Superhero on the line. I know he's there and I want to talk to him."

Edie handed the phone to Jack without a word. She buried her head in her hands and sobbed. She was shivering like the temperature was fifteen degrees even though it was comfortably warm in Jack's kitchen.

Jack gently squeezed her shoulders to no response as he placed the phone to his ear. "What kind of slimy bastard involves a child in something like this?"

"The kind that means business. Don't you forget that."

"You listen to me, you sick son of a bitch," he said, his voice a guttural growl. "If anything happens to that little girl you had better grow eyes in the back of your head, because I will never stop looking until I find you. And once I find you, I'll never stop coming at you until I slit your throat and let you watch yourself die."

Gravel Voice seemed unimpressed. "Blah, blah, blah. Empty threats, Mr. Sheridan. Now it's my turn to talk, so pay attention. You have exactly one week to complete the job as outlined in your email. Your clock starts now."

"I already know that."

"Then know this: when you've performed to our satisfaction, we will provide details on where and how to pick up Janie. Get the job done quickly, Ms. Tolliver gets her child back quickly. The length of time that poor mother suffers is entirely up to you. But consider this your very own trigger warning. A literal one. Do not even think about fucking with us. Do so and that little girl gets two 9mm slugs in the head. Do you understand me?"

Jack couldn't remember the last time he'd been this angry. He doubted he ever had. He wanted to crawl through the telephone line and rip Gravel Voice's eyes out of his head and shove them down his throat. Wanted to beat him to a pulp with his bare hands.

But he forced himself to remain calm. Janie's life was at stake.

"Yes, I understand," he said. "But I have one demand, and it is non-negotiable."

"Is that so?"

"Yes, it's so. Edie Tolliver will be permitted to speak with her child every day, without exception, until the assignment is complete. If so much as one day goes by without her talking to Janie, the deal is off."

"It seems you still don't understand your position in the pecking order, Mr. Sheridan. We hold up the hoops and you jump through them. Period."

"That may be," Jack said, speaking through a jaw clenched so tight the pain radiated into his skull, "but the first day that goes by without Ms. Tolliver hearing from her little girl, the agreement is off and you can kill Jim Studds yourself. I'll be too busy hunting your sorry ass down to do it for you. Do *you* understand *me*?"

"Enough is enough. You've gotten your proof of life. You'd better get to work or Little Miss Blondie will never see her snot-nosed brat again."

"And you'd better call here tomorrow, or you'll never be able to breathe easily again."

The line went dead.

Jack held the phone in hands shaking with rage.

He set it down and knelt next to Edie. Her head was still buried in her hands.

He lifted her chin gently, forcing her to look at him. "You did a great job."

She shook her head. "I forgot to tell them to call every day."

"You were outstanding," he repeated. "I didn't mind passing along that little message myself. I only asked you to do it because I wasn't sure whether I'd get to talk to them."

She nodded dully. Her eyes were glazed and she lay limply against the kitchen wall. Talking to Janie seemed to have sapped all her energy.

"They *will* call here tomorrow, and you *will* get another chance to talk to Janie. And I'll get her back to you. I promise you that."

She nodded again and closed her eyes. She looked exhausted.

Jack slipped one arm under her knees and the other under her lower back and lifted her gently off the floor. He carried her to the couch and placed her on it before covering her with a blanket.

"Try to get some sleep," he said. "Nothing's going to happen for a while, and I'll be across the room at the computer if you need me."

Edie coughed out a bitter laugh. "I won't be able to sleep. There's no way I'll sleep again until I have my baby back in my arms."

Then she closed her eyes and was gone.

# 16

Jack didn't have the slightest inkling as to the specifics of *Mole*'s operation, nor had he ever had reason to care until about an hour ago. Ron Earl had tried to give him a quick and dirty rundown of the program's basics upon delivery—something about infiltrating protected ISPs and back-tracing hidden addresses—but he'd stopped as soon as he came to the realization every word was going straight over Jack's head.

Now Jack wished he'd paid a little more attention.

Supposedly the software had been designed to be user-friendly to non-computer experts, but Ron and the rest of the design team hadn't wasted any effort developing the fancy graphics or pretty bells and whistles that would have been required had *Mole* been intended for public use.

After easing Edie onto the couch and trudging back to his computer, Jack touched his mouse to remove the screensaver. Filling his monitor was a *Mole* screen consisting mostly of a series of numbers and symbols, none of which meant a damned thing to Jack.

The top of the screen was dominated by a banner announcing: MOLE IS IDENTIFYING ORIGINATION, DO NOT EXIT PROGRAM. A rudimentary status bar ran across the bottom of the screen. The status bar did nothing to instill confidence in Jack that *Mole* was identifying anything, the optimistic statement at the top of the screen notwithstanding. The status bar was barely one-third filled in and seemed to be moving at a glacial pace.

He sighed and rubbed his eyes. They were grainy and dry. It felt much later than five-thirty in the afternoon. He glanced across the room and noticed Edie had kicked off her blanket. She mumbled something in her sleep and then fell silent again.

When he returned his attention to the monitor he almost wished he hadn't. Nothing had changed. The banner at the top continued to radiate optimism, while the status bar at the bottom insisted on dashing it.

Jack pushed out his chair, moving slowly to avoid waking Edie, and walked into the kitchen to put on some coffee. This had the makings of a very long night.

# 17

Edie was running as fast as she could. She was sprinting but didn't know why.

She didn't know where she was going.

She didn't know anything except that it was critically important she run.

The landscape surrounding her was bleak. It was nightfall and she was on the side of a secluded road and the trees were bare and skeletal. They danced on an invisible breeze and their branches reached for her with bony fingers, and the fingers were accusatory, but of what she did not know.

No houses lined the lonely road. Not a soul was in sight.

She was utterly alone.

Edie continued to run without knowing why. It was odd that she wasn't getting tired considering the speed she maintained.

She wracked her brain, trying to determine what she was running toward. Or was she running away? There didn't seem to be anyone or anything chasing her, but the road was winding and hilly and there was no way to be sure.

Something was picking at her brain, at the edges of her consciousness, but the more she tried to focus on it, the more the specifics eluded her. It was as if—

A cry in the distance snapped her out of her reverie. The sound was plaintive and somehow familiar, and without knowing why, Edie picked up her already frantic pace. She *had* to hurry.

As she ran, the cries came again and again, desperate and needy and ever more strident.

And then she knew.

The cries were coming from Janie, and her little girl was terrified and maybe even injured and she needed her mommy and Edie *had to get to her.*

Somehow she put on a burst of speed. Now she knew she was running *toward* something, and that something was holding her baby, and while she didn't know *what* was holding her baby, she did know this: nothing would stop her from getting to Janie now that she understood her purpose.

She ran on, Janie's voice becoming clearer with each pounding step. "Mommy help me, please Mommy, help meeee…"

But where was her little girl? The voice was frightened but loud and clear; she should be *right here.* Edie looked in all directions and saw nothing, only the skeletal trees and the gathering darkness.

Then she looked skyward in frustration, and when she did she froze.

Stopped running in mid-stride, stumbling in the process and nearly falling to the pavement.

Stared in silent terror as a vulture circled overhead. It was massive, the size of a circus elephant if not larger. Its wingspan was easily twenty feet and when it flapped those grotesquely large wings, Edie could hear a sound like a giant flag whipping in a strong wind.

The vulture was much too big to be real, and yet there it was. It wheeled and darted in the sky but never strayed, remaining directly above Edie, staring down at her with cold bloodshot reptilian eyes.

The creature was terrifying, but after her first glance Edie barely noticed it.

Because trapped in its claws was her child.

Janie.

For a long moment Edie was unable to move, unable even to breathe, shocked into inaction by the sight of her baby girl hanging limp and helpless high above the pavement. Blood dripped with metronome-like regularity from the bird's talons. It was Janie's blood, and it splattered onto the road, each drop sounding as loud in Edie's ears as the *crack* of a rifle shot.

And then Edie got her breath back.

She screamed in helpless agony at the hideous creature, "Take me, take me, please take me, put my baby down and take me instead," and then she was crying and screaming and cursing and leaping at the vulture but it was too high, it was so high and it was holding her baby, and then the creature was pecking at Janie, opening gash after gash in her skull, and the blood was falling to the pavement in a steady flow, and Edie's legs let go, they were unable to hold her upright any longer and she dropped to the ground, and then without warning the creature released Janie, and her tiny little-girl body plummeted toward the pavement, and—

And the ground was shaking as her daughter's falling body blurred and became insubstantial in her vision and then faded away entirely.

But the ground continued shaking, the tremors getting stronger and stronger, and then her eyes fluttered open and after a moment's sheer confusion reality clicked into place.

The ground wasn't shaking and she wasn't lying on the pavement. No vulture circled overhead. She was prone on Jack's couch, exactly where he'd placed her after the phone call from the awful man who'd taken Janie. Jack hovered over her, one hand on her shoulder shaking her awake, his touch gentle, concern evident in his worried expression.

Edie's heart melted.

She should hate Jack Sheridan. Up until just now she'd thought she *did* hate him. He was the not the man she'd thought she was falling in love with, that much was obvious.

And now Janie was gone and he was to blame.

She'd made clear her revulsion at all he'd revealed. She had been cold and hard as she tried to process the loss of both her daughter and her new boyfriend. He was not a stupid man; he had to know she could never be with someone who assassinated people for a living, even if those people were the worst sorts of criminals.

But despite everything he held her as she suffered, rocking her out of her nightmare with heartbreak in his eyes and unfathomable gentleness in his manner. He was broken by the knowledge that he was responsible for Janie's disappearance and Edie's suffering. Guilt radiated from him, leaking through every pore like a disease.

And although Edie now questioned everything she thought she knew about this man, one thing remained clear: he stood ready to risk his life—to give it if necessary—to return her child to her arms. Because sharing space with the heartbreak in his eyes was a steely resolve.

Jack Sheridan would get Janie back or die trying.

Edie ran her fingers through her tangle of hair and shook her head groggily. Her mouth tasted like she hadn't brushed her teeth in six months.

"How long was I asleep?" she croaked.

"Not long. Maybe half an hour."

"What's happening with your tracer program?"

He shrugged. "Hard to say. It's doing something, so I guess I can assume that's a good sign. It's a slog, though. According to the developer, it has to analyze algorithms or something and that takes time. I don't claim to understand the process, but until I get a notification that the tracer has failed, I'm going to assume it's working."

Edie removed Jack's hand from her shoulder, giving it a barely perceptible squeeze as she let go, then she sat up. Her head was pounding from stress and the disorientation of a thirty-minute nap when she needed so much more. But she wasn't complaining; she would have bet a week's Three Squares Diner receipts that she couldn't fall asleep under the circumstances.

"What can I do to help?" she said. She perched on the edge of the couch and looked up at Jack expectantly.

"Nothing at the moment. All we can do is wait." Jack grabbed a second pillow from the other end of the couch and slipped it behind her.

He tried to ease her back down and said, "You might as well get some more sleep. You're going to need your strength."

"No," she answered, stiffening against his touch. "I can't sleep anymore. I don't want to sleep anymore. I want my baby back. That's all I want in the world. I would gladly give anything to get her back, including myself."

"I know."

"I can't live without her, Jack. Get my little girl back. Please."

"That's exactly what we're going to do."

# 18

Bradley Chilcott sipped scotch from a too-large tumbler as he sat behind the desk in his home office. Across the room a fire crackled in the gas fireplace and he watched, entranced, as the flames danced and leapt.

It was really too late in the year for a fire, even a small one regulated by the remote-control rheostat he kept on the corner of the desk. The temperature inside the office was rising uncomfortably, but Bradley didn't care. He'd always been fascinated by fire, by its ability to consume virtually anything, and he found watching the flames to be more relaxing than anything else he'd ever tried, including alcohol and drugs.

Although he had to admit alcohol came in a close second.

He really needed that relaxation right now. The plan he and Hargus had spent so long developing was finally in motion, transforming from idle chatter into real—and felonious—action. And now that events were underway, Bradley wanted them over and done with, the sooner the better.

He glanced at his watch without absorbing the time. What did it matter? He'd been checking the damned thing roughly every three minutes for the last several hours, and the whole exercise was pointless anyway. The end result of the strategy he and Mike had executed would not become clear for several days at least.

Assuming Jack Sheridan did as he was told—and he would have no choice, since Bradley and Mike had trapped him so securely in their web—it wasn't like Jim Studds would suddenly turn up dead overnight. Even a top-flight professional assassin wasn't a miracle worker.

And based on what Bradley had read in the CIA's supposedly Top Secret Jack Sheridan file, the man defined the phrase "top flight." He was one of the most effective and efficient operators the Central Intelligence Agency had ever seen.

He was the best of the best.

Which was exactly why Bradley had insisted on utilizing Sheridan, overruling that pussy Hargus's strongly worded objections. Hargus's argument had gone something like, "We want someone good, obviously, but Sheridan is *too good*. He's too smart. Too clever. If we use this guy and anything goes wrong, anything at all, we'll end up roasting on the end of a stick in Jack Sheridan's campfire."

It was a ridiculous argument and Bradley had let Hargus know it, in no uncertain terms. Bradley Chilcott deserved the best, in all areas of his life. If Sheridan was the cream of the crop it was all the *more* reason to force him to carry out the mission, not an excuse for passing him over.

Everything was going to work out just fine. He knew it would because everything *always* worked out fine for Bradley Chilcott. It was good breeding, or outstanding preparation, or just plain dumb luck, but things had been working out just fine for Bradley as long as he could remember.

This little adventure would be no exception.

But if that were the case, why did he feel so uneasy? Why was he sitting next to his phone like a twelve-year-old girl waiting for a call from her crush?

He took another sip of his drink, then muttered, "Ah, what the hell," and turned it into a gulp. He wanted—needed—something to take his mind off the impending end of Jim Studds's political career. And life.

He wondered what Mike Hargus was doing right now.

Wondered what Jack Sheridan was doing right now.

The tension was killing him. He wondered if this was how Machiavelli had felt as he manipulated people, bending them to his will and forcing events to fit his agenda.

The sensation wasn't just nerve-wracking; it was exhilarating.

It was intoxicating.

It was arousing.

Bradley realized he was hard as a rock. Throbbing and as horny as he'd probably ever been since he was seventeen years old. Suddenly he wanted nothing more than to be naked and inside the little "conference room" located down the hall from his office at the State House.

Technically it was a large service closet, or at least it had been prior to the Studds/Chilcott administration. But shortly after taking office, Bradley had had all of the janitor's supplies hauled out of the closet. He'd refurbished it—using taxpayer funds, of course, but what was the point of having power if you couldn't wield it for yourself every once in a while?—with a small but comfortable bed and brand new mattress, a small but high-quality television with a DVD player suitable for watching porn, even a small but well-stocked bar.

In the years since taking office, Bradley had utilized his little love nest more times than he could count. Occasionally he relaxed in it alone but most often entertained young, star-struck political groupies, interns, or even staff members.

He always got a rush thinking about the legendary tunnel JFK had supposedly used to sneak Marilyn Monroe into and out of the White House. When all the skullduggery was over and he'd ascended to the presidency, he vowed to reopen Kennedy's tunnel.

Over the years, Bradley had learned to be extremely cautious, his State House love nest notwithstanding. Sex with underage girls—and especially sex that involved *hitting* underage girls—was generally frowned upon, even inside the cosmopolitan, progressive D.C. Beltway. Bradley knew that if his unusual sexual appetites were to become public knowledge, voters would run screaming to any other candidate on Election Day.

His lifelong dream of becoming president of the United States would be rendered moot. So would his freedom, most likely. He would never win another election and would spend a good portion of the rest of his life in prison.

God knew he had spent enough money paying off families to ensure that did not happen.

He sipped/gulped his drink again and thought about Kim. It

wasn't that he didn't care for his wife. Of course he did, although calling what he felt for her *love* would probably not be accurate. Bradley doubted he was capable of actually *loving* anyone other than himself.

But the notion of a man like Bradley Chilcott, with his oversized appetites and grand plans, limiting himself to just one woman for the rest of his life, even if she was beautiful and accomplished and loyal, was just ridiculous.

It was unrealistic.

It wasn't going to happen.

The marriage had been a sham right from the start. The first time Kim caught him with another woman was barely six weeks after they'd taken their vows. Hell, it happened so quickly, he hadn't even hit her yet for the first time.

*But it wasn't my fault, goddammit.*

His face flushed with anger and humiliation, even now, years later, as he recalled the circumstances surrounding that moment.

Kim was supposed to be working. She'd left in the morning just like she always did, after making Bradley his breakfast and coffee and kissing him goodbye.

He'd told her he was going to work from home, which had surprised her. Both of them held roughly the same lowly staff positions in the D.C. offices of the Democrat from Massachusetts and the Republican from Georgia, and working from home was certainly not any kind of option for Kim. But she had accepted his story on the blind faith of the newly married and gone off to work.

Bradley, of course, did not have the option of working from home any more than Kim did. He'd called in sick because one of the cute little secretaries in the senator's office had made quite clear the sorts of things she wanted to do to Bradley, and he'd easily convinced her to call in sick as well.

Two hours later Kim returned home, supposedly because she felt ill. The traitorous bitch walked in on Bradley and the little secretary performing duties in the bedroom that were most definitely not related to official Senate business.

The situation had been difficult for Bradley at the time, but looking back on it now, he realized everything had worked out for the best. There would have been no point in stringing Kim along, in making her believe their relationship was anything more than a fiction to be maintained for the sake of Bradley's career.

In a way, he'd done her a favor.

After an initial period of...adjustment...Kim had dutifully maintained that fiction. Whether for the sake of the career she still at that point envisioned having, or out of love for Bradley, or perhaps because in her own way she enjoyed the perks that came with being one of the Chosen Few in a country where millions of people actually believed that "all men are created equal" drivel written into the Declaration of Independence, Kim Chilcott stayed by her husband's side.

Through serial affairs, serial beatings, and the humiliation of knowing her husband viewed her as nothing more than a prop designed to attract voters, Kim Chilcott stayed.

Bradley snickered at the thought. He wasn't sure whether he admired or despised his wife for the choices she'd made. Ultimately, of course, it was irrelevant, a distinction without a difference. Because the pretty wife and fresh-faced children served his purposes exactly as he'd always known they would.

And nothing else mattered.

He lifted the tumbler to his lips and grimaced when he discovered he'd drained the glass and four mostly melted ice cubes were all that remained.

Time for more scotch.

He stretched and sighed as he pushed himself to his feet. Without thinking he rechecked his watch.

He wondered yet again what Jack Sheridan was doing, whether the assassin they'd lured into their trap had finalized his plan for killing Jim Studds.

Doing so wouldn't get him the little girl back, of course. Nothing would. It was unfortunate but necessary that she disappear forever the moment Studds was dead.

Sheridan wouldn't have any way of knowing that, of course.

So Bradley had no doubt the supposedly brilliant assassin was even now working feverishly to complete his mission. And that thought made him happy, despite his growing suspicion that this time he may have bitten off more than he could chew.

# 19

Edie had fallen asleep again. For a while Jack replaced the blanket each time she kicked it off, but eventually he decided he was fighting a losing battle and gave up trying.

Her sleep was restless and tortured, but at least she wasn't screaming again.

For now.

Every few seconds he glanced at his computer monitor, willing *Mole* to work faster. His wishes were having no effect on the program, though, and he found himself spending most of his time watching his girlfriend—his now *ex*-girlfriend, he supposed—try to sleep.

There could be no doubt their relationship was over. He had lied to her about his profession, had been responsible for her only child being kidnapped and threatened with violent death, and had admitted to her that he was ready to go outside the law—*way* outside, in fact—to effect her return.

He couldn't imagine any woman getting past all that, much less one with as strong a sense of personal morality as Edie Tolliver.

There was even the possibility she would turn him in to the authorities. Jack wouldn't blame her if she did. He didn't even care at this point, as long as she didn't drop the dime until after he'd gotten Janie back.

Behind him the computer beeped twice. The sound was unexpected and jarring against the otherwise unbroken silence inside the house.

After what felt like hours of staring at his mostly unchanging monitor, Jack was suddenly reluctant to check on the significance of what was obviously an internal program alarm. If *Mole* was unsuccessful in tracing the kidnappers' threatening email, he had no idea what he was going to do next.

Everything was riding on the tech genius of Ron Earl.

Jack sighed deeply and swiveled in his chair to face the music.

\*　\*　\*

*Mole*'s report was longer and more detailed than Jack had expected. It included reams of statistics, most of which were meaningless to him.

But one thing became immediately obvious: the kidnappers had gone to extraordinary lengths to hide their identities. The email in question had been routed through nine separate secure servers located in six different countries around the globe. It had been encrypted using some of the latest and most sophisticated encryption techniques.

The overall level of sophistication suggested that at least one of the kidnappers had at some point been involved—and, like Jack, still maintained connections inside—the intelligence community. Ordinary citizens, even computer experts capable of carrying out complex hacking attacks, could not typically manage what the kidnappers had accomplished.

But as sophisticated as the encryption and routing had been, it was still no match for *Mole*. Jack skimmed over the statistical analysis, looking for the only thing he really cared about: the identity of email's originator.

He found it toward the end of the report.

The owner of the account that had sent the email regarding Janie Tolliver's kidnapping, and demanding the murder of Maryland Governor Jim Studds, was someone so unsurprising and obvious Jack was angry he hadn't thought of it immediately: Maryland *Lieutenant* Governor, Bradley Chilcott.

It made sense in a sick, twisted way. Who would be more

invested in bumping off the Number One Guy than his under-study? It was a tale as old as time: the head man gets rubbed out by the person next in line.

But there had to be more to the story. Politicians might be bloodthirsty and ruthless—*were* usually bloodthirsty and ruthless, in Jack's opinion—but lieutenant governors generally did not possess the means to manage a scenario like this one without the assistance of someone with extensive experience in areas even more rough-and-tumble than politics.

He sat quietly, pondering the connections between human nature and power and murder. He considered the type of person who would be capable of executing a plan so ruthless it involved the cold-blooded execution of not just a politician, but an innocent little girl.

He was so engrossed in his thoughts he didn't notice Edie had awakened. She stood directly behind him and gazed intently over his shoulder at the computer screen. He jumped in surprise at her light touch on his back, and then reached out instinctively to hold her around her waist before realizing that contact in such a familiar way was no longer his right.

He withdrew his arm, wondering if she noticed. If she did, she didn't mention it.

She didn't say anything for a while.

Neither of them did.

Eventually she nodded at the screen and said, "Who the hell is Bradley Chilcott?"

# 20

A couple of hours online revealed all that was publically available regarding Maryland Lieutenant Governor Bradley Chilcott.

He'd been raised in a well-to-do D.C. family.

Georgetown University grad.

Pretty wife.

Two young children.

Everything in Chilcott's background pointed to a man with big ambitions who'd spent every waking moment of his life preparing for a political career on the Big Stage. A man who'd likely teamed up as the understudy on a gubernatorial ticket with wildly popular Jim Studds with the expectation that the aging Studds would serve no more than a single term, allowing Chilcott to slide into the governor's office.

But that same two hours on the Internet revealed that Studds had shocked everyone involved in Maryland politics just weeks ago by announcing his intention to run for a second term in the fall, thus dooming the upwardly mobile Bradley Chilcott to four more years languishing in obscurity.

The scenario provided plenty of motivation for a ruthless man to contemplate murder. Jack had seen people killed for much less.

He'd started his search operation under the premise that Bradley Chilcott might be a dupe, that the same people who'd kidnapped Janie in order to blackmail Jack into committing murder could be setting up Chilcott to take the fall if their plan went south.

But twenty minutes into his search, Jack abandoned that

premise for two reasons. First, the kidnappers had done such a thorough job of covering their tracks by routing the email through so many secure servers that they had to assume the message would never be traced back to its point of origination. And it was a valid assumption. If not for *Mole*, the CIA/NSA's Top Secret program, they *would* have been safe.

Second, the more details regarding Bradley Chilcott the Internet search revealed, the more they seemed to fit with a man willing to go to extraordinary lengths to get ahead. There had been persistent rumors of dalliances between the lieutenant governor and underage girls, reported only in less-than-reputable newspapers and sketchy blogs, but on enough occasions to convince Jack that there had to be something to the story.

*Where there's smoke, there's fire* wasn't a cliché for nothing.

The same less-than-reputable news sources had hinted at Chilcott possibly enjoying violent encounters with his partners. They whispered about payoffs, and intimidation of the girls and their families, and painted a chilling picture of Bradley Chilcott, not just as a politician but as a man and a human being.

"Reputable" news sources had scrupulously avoided any mention of the whispered allegations, a situation that served only to intensify Jack's conviction that they were likely true. Politicians and their staffs were notorious for tightly controlling their narratives, and if Chilcott was comfortable using bribes and strong-arm tactics with witnesses in potentially criminal situations, it didn't take any great stretch of imagination to think he might use the same tactics on reporters and news outlets.

All of which proved nothing, of course. As reprehensible as the stories would make Bradley Chilcott if true, Jack suspected the man would have plenty of company when it came to exhibiting sociopathic tendencies within the political arena.

And none of what Jack found online necessarily proved Chilcott was a man capable of orchestrating murder. It was still a big leap between sexual deviance and resorting to hardline tactics to cover up that deviance, and conspiring to kidnap a child in order to force the assassination of a sitting governor.

But within two hours of beginning his research, with an impatient Edie pacing behind him and voicing her displeasure at the delay while her child was missing, Jack had decided there were no other reasonable alternative theories that would fit with Janie's abduction and the awful contents of the email that had been sent by one Bradley A. Chilcott.

Once he'd satisfied himself as to Chilcott's involvement, the next step was to delve into the lieutenant governor's personal and professional connections.

The first assumption Jack made while doing so was that while Bradley Chilcott was the point of origination for the conspiracy, his involvement was almost certainly limited to behind-the scenes maneuvering. The notion that a sitting state lieutenant governor would be able to drive or fly to New Hampshire, kidnap a seven-year-old, and then take her into hiding was absurd.

Given that assumption, Jack decided to begin researching those closest to Chilcott. He eliminated the wife from consideration almost immediately and decided to return to her only if research into Chilcott's political connections turned up nothing. It seemed highly unlikely Kim Chilcott would be involved in something as sordid as the kidnapping of a young girl, especially given the fact she had children of her own that were close to the same age as the victim.

So who would a political mover and shaker trust with such a brutal conspiracy?

Jack brought up his Internet search engine and used it to uncover a flow chart listing the official rungs on the ladder of Maryland's state government. A plot like the one Chilcott had undertaken would require extensive planning. It would involve multiple meetings and communications. Thus the actual kidnapper had to be someone close to Chilcott professionally, someone who could meet with the man daily if necessary and not raise suspicion doing so.

The number of people working on a lieutenant governor's staff who would have the kind of virtually unlimited access to the man that the kidnapping plot would require, was relatively small.

It didn't take long for Jack to focus on one name: Chilcott's Director of Security, Mike Hargus.

Jack was by no means a political junkie. He voted in elections and possessed strongly-held beliefs regarding the role of government in the lives of its citizens, but the more he knew about the day-to-day operation of that government, the less respect he tended to have for the men and women who ran it.

He'd decided long ago to devote what little free time and energy he had into something—anything—other than monitoring the political process. So his unfamiliarity with the duties of a state lieutenant governor, and the staff required to fulfill those duties, was virtually absolute.

That said, the title "Director of Security" stuck out like a sore thumb among all the others populating Chilcott's staff flow chart. Without exception, the other jobs were bland and colorless, exactly what one might expect to see when examining the nuts and bolts operation of the bureaucratic process.

And who better to carry out the dirty work of paying off and intimidating witnesses, if the stories Jack had read in the less-than-reputable news sources and blogs were even partially true, than a "Director of Security?"

And if *that* were true, it required only a small leap of logic to imagine the same man being capable of carrying out the politically motivated kidnapping of a child.

The lieutenant governor's director of security could meet with his boss at any time. He could do so often as he liked without raising an eyebrow of suspicion among onlookers.

It didn't take long for Jack to decide Hargus was the man he was looking for.

Furthermore, he almost instantly began to get a very bad feeling in the pit of his stomach when he started researching Chilcott's director of security. The Internet references to him from 2010, when he began working full-time for Chilcott, until late-spring 2016, were more or less what one would expect of a man whose job was to remain mostly in the shadows. His name popped up sporadically but on a semi-regular basis.

But online references to Mike Hargus for the previous twenty-three years—from 1987 until his 2010 hiring by Bradley Chilcott—were nonexistent.

The search turned up nothing.

Literally.

Jack found occasional references prior to 1987 regarding a

Mike Hargus who'd been born in 1970 and raised in New Jersey. He decided it had to be the same guy, because the last name was so unusual and the age fit with the small bio of Hargus included on the Maryland State government website.

Mike Hargus had grown up in Newark and lived there through his 1987 high school graduation. He appeared in a local newspaper story after making a critical error in a New Jersey high school baseball playoff game. He appeared again in the papers following a couple of scrapes with the Newark Police—nothing major, juvenile delinquency stuff like breaking and entering and public drunkenness—and then, following his graduation, he'd disappeared.

Completely.

It was like the man vanished into thin air for almost a quarter-century.

This was a very bad sign. The lack of public information was strikingly similar to what a Google search of Jack's own name would turn up, in fact, minus Hargus's scrapes with the police.

The only explanation for how a man could exist in modern-day America and still remain invisible electronically concerned Jack. It also convinced him he was on the right track when it came to pinpointing the kidnappers.

Mike Hargus had been an intelligence operator, exactly as Jack had been.

It would make sense. An operator whose moral compass had rotted away would be perfectly suited to carrying out the kinds of jobs a dirty politician would require of his security director.

He would be perfectly suited to kidnapping and holding hostage a young child.

He would be someone Chilcott might feel comfortable approaching with a plot to assassinate a sitting governor.

Jack sat back in his chair, conscious of Edie's growing impatience but knowing he stood no chance of effecting Janie's return if he charged off in the wrong direction. He thought about rogue operators, and child kidnappers, and men so desperate for power they would be willing to commit cold-blooded murder to achieve it.

He was on the right track. He could feel it.

But right now, all he had were suspicions. He needed more.

He bent back over his computer keyboard and began typing, searching until he found the telephone number he wanted.

Then he picked up the phone and punched in the digits.

# 21

Jack checked his watch. It was after six.

Not much after six, but still, it was after six.

*Dammit.*

He had no idea how late Maryland state house offices stayed open, but he doubted it was past five.

He listened to the buzz of the line ringing in his ear and wondered what he would do if no one answered. He really wanted confirmation that Hargus was his guy before he went any further, but the prospect of waiting another fifteen hours to get that confirmation was unacceptable. He couldn't afford that much down time. Not with Janie missing and Jack operating under the kidnappers' strict timetable.

*Buzz.*

*Buzz.*

He blew out a breath in frustration. He would have to hang up and—

"Hello, you've reached the office of Maryland Lieutenant Governor Bradley Chilcott. My name is Amanda, how may I help you?"

Jack was so surprised he almost forgot to answer.

"Hello? Is anyone there?" The voice sounded young but competent, and Jack guessed he was about to be hung up on.

"Yes, hello. I'm sorry, I didn't really expect anyone to be in the office at this hour."

He could hear the smile in her voice when she replied. "I get that a lot when people call at this time of day. Yet it doesn't stop them from trying! I'm an intern. I work in Lieutenant Governor Chilcott's office for credit toward my graduate degree in Political Science, and the lieutenant governor was kind enough to allow me to build my hours working in his office after classes and my part-time job."

*Kindness has nothing to do with it,* Jack thought. *You'd better be very careful, Amanda the Intern, because you're probably next on the slimeball's Pretty Girl Hit Parade, with the operative word being "hit."*

"So…how can I help you?"

Jack realized he'd fallen silent again and mentally kicked himself. He affected what he hoped was a clipped, professional tone and said, "Well, the lieutenant governor's kindness has definitely worked in my favor tonight. I'll have to thank him the next time I see him."

"You know Lieutenant Governor Chilcott?"

"Only in passing. My name is Ted Sanders, and I'm a journalist. Our paths have crossed once or twice, though I doubt a man as busy as the lieutenant governor would remember it as well as I do."

"Ted Sanders…" The intern repeated the name slowly. It was obvious she was jotting it down. "I'm sorry Mr. Sanders, but the lieutenant governor is gone for the day. In fact, I'm the only one left in the office. Do you have a message you'd like me to pass along, or a number at which the lieutenant governor can reach you tomorrow?"

"No ma'am, a call back won't be necessary," Jack said. "I actually don't need to speak with Lieutenant Governor Chilcott at all. I know how valuable his time is and don't want to bother him, but I'm hoping that as one of his staffers, perhaps you could assist me."

"Of course. I'll help if I can."

"Excellent. I think I mentioned I'm a journalist…"

"Yes, you did. I considered majoring in journalism but ultimately decided to enter the field of politics. I really want to help people, you know, like Lieutenant Governor Chilcott does."

Jack shook his head. *Good Lord, Amanda the Intern, you don't stand a chance against a shark like Chilcott.*

"Yes, journalism definitely has its moments," he answered. "Anyway, I'm currently working on a contract assignment for The New Yorker magazine. I assume you've heard of it?"

"The New Yorker? Of course. How exciting! What can I help you with?"

"The subject of the piece is the challenges faced by those charged with protecting public figures in the era of lone wolf terrorism. As such, I was hoping to schedule an appointment to speak with the lieutenant governor's director of security. That would be a man named…"

He pretended to search his notes.

"Ah! Here we are. I'd like to schedule an appointment to speak with Mike Hargus at his earliest convenience. Tomorrow if possible. I'm on an extremely tight deadline," he said.

No answer.

"You know editors," he added with a conspiratorial chuckle designed to make Amanda the Intern feel like an insider, even though Jack was quite certain she didn't "know editors" any better than he did.

"Ohhhh," she said slowly.

"Is there a problem?"

"Well, I don't know Mr. Hargus very well, but I get the feeling he doesn't really like being in the spotlight." Her tone changed the moment Jack mentioned Hargus's name. She was afraid of him. Her fear was as clear to Jack as if she had shouted the words through the phone.

"Oh, that's no problem," he reassured her. "All I need is some generic info, maybe some broad background material. If Mr. Hargus prefers not to be quoted directly, I'll be happy to protect his privacy by keeping his words anonymous. And I've never given up a confidential source in all my years on the job," he said proudly.

*Hell, it's even true.*

"Well, I'm afraid there's another problem, and it might be a deal-breaker if you're on a tight deadline."

*Now we're getting somewhere.* "Really? What problem would that be?"

"Mr. Hargus is currently unavailable. I'm told he'll be out of the office for about a week."

"Oh?"

"Yes. Lieutenant Governor Chilcott told Mr. Hargus that he's been working too hard and insisted he take a week off. I'm not sure where he went—camping, maybe?—but I do know that Mr. Hargus won't be in the area for the next several days. My understanding is that he's unreachable, even by cell phone."

*Camping.*

*For a week.*

"Well, that's a shame," he said, feigning disappointment. "I guess I'll have to touch base with security people for some other public figures. Thanks very much for your assistance, though, Amanda. I very much appreciate you taking the time to help me."

"I'm afraid I didn't help you at all."

"Oh, that's not true. You helped me far more than you realize."

"I'm so glad!" The voice that had gotten wary and frightened at the mention of Mike Hargus became bright and chipper again, and Jack felt sorry for the girl. He guessed she was going to get plenty of experience over the course of her internship, but that very little of it would be beneficial.

She said, "Are you sure you wouldn't like a call back from the lieutenant governor?"

"That won't be necessary," Jack said. "But thank you. I'm sure I'll be seeing Lieutenant Governor Chilcott very soon anyway. I'll introduce myself personally when that happens."

"Don't you mean reintroduce yourself?"

"Yes, of course. Reintroduce myself. But I'd like it to be a surprise when that happens, and since I wasn't able to connect with Mr. Hargus for my magazine piece, I would prefer you not mention my call to the lieutenant governor."

"Oh. Okay."

"Thanks so much."

"No problem! You have a nice night now, Mr. Sanders."

"You too, Amanda. And thanks again."

Jack disconnected the call and looked up to find Edie staring at him, her eyes burning with intensity.

"Well?" she said.

"I know where to start."

"Then let's get to it."

# 22

Jack thought for a while that he was going to have to chain Edie to her chair. "I'm going with you," she insisted doggedly.

He'd slept—sort of—on the couch overnight after insisting Edie take his bed. She claimed to have gotten a decent night's sleep, but he didn't believe her. Her face was haggard, and dark half-moons under her eyes testified to the lie. It was eight a.m. and she looked as though she'd been awake all night.

He shook his head firmly. "There's nothing you can do to help me. And besides, you have a much more important job to handle."

"What could possibly be more important than helping you get Janie back?"

"She's going to call every day, remember? You have to be here to talk to her, to reassure her that everything's going to be okay."

Edie instantly teared up and the now-familiar sense of guilt and shame wrapped itself a little more tightly around Jack's soul.

"What if they don't let her call?" she whispered.

"She'll call," Jack said firmly. "I made it clear the deal was off if we went even one day without hearing from her. So don't worry about that."

She still looked doubtful.

"Janie will call," he repeated. "Besides, I'll be back soon. And when I arrive, we'll have made significant progress toward getting Janie back where she belongs: with her mother."

He hoped he wasn't deceiving her again.

# 23

Jack had briefly considered flying to Newark. In the end, though, he decided that if he left at the right time of day—planning his trip so that rush hour was just ending as he skirted Boston—he could drive his truck to Jersey and make it almost as quickly.

It would be worth what little time he lost because he hated to fly. He did it all the time, thanks to the nature of his work, but he still hated it. Long security lines, weather delays, traffic delays, unsatisfying service, they all contributed to Jack's determination to drive whenever possible.

There was one more reason Jack preferred his truck to any airplane: in a post-9/11 world, smuggling a handgun onto a commercial flight required more effort than he was willing to expend toward the proposition. And even though he didn't expect to *need* a weapon today, he wasn't prepared to bet his life on that expectation.

So at a little after eight a.m., he tossed a small bag into his truck and aimed south. A couple of miles to get to Interstate 93, and then at a steady seventy mile per hour pace—barring any unexpected backups due to accidents or construction, both of which were always a possibility—he would roll into Newark before midafternoon.

Leaving Edie alone in her current terrified state was not ideal, but allowing her to accompany him simply was not an option. The closer he got to recovering Janie, the more dangerous the mission would become, and he'd already done enough damage to her little family as it was. He couldn't bear the thought of being responsible for destroying her life any more than he'd already done.

That was the real reason he'd insisted the kidnappers call every day. He was convinced they would not harm a hair on Janie's head as long as she served their purposes, but he also knew without question they would eliminate her the minute she became a liability: when Jim Studds was dead.

Thus, the daily phone calls were not strictly necessary. But Jack couldn't begin to imagine how Edie must be suffering. Asking her to spend as many as seven days trapped inside his tiny house, pacing and terrified, imagining the worst possible outcome for her child, was hard enough with the knowledge she could speak with Janie every day.

Asking her to do it without that reassurance would be cruelty of the highest magnitude.

And Edie would have nothing to occupy her time. She'd already arranged for Chief Cook Mark Goetz to take over the day-to-day operations of The Three Squares Diner for the next week. Mark was hardworking and trustworthy and had been with Edie since the day the diner had opened.

She told him nothing more than that she needed to take a little time off, and to his credit he'd not asked a single question.

* * *

The drive seemed to take forever. Jack ran into no significant traffic backups, but being alone in the truck, with only his regrets for company, made the time drag.

Normally he would listen to music, especially if on an assignment. It helped relieve the stifling tension that was as much a part of his career field as breathing.

But this was not a music situation. He didn't *want* to relieve the tension. He wanted to feel every last ounce of weight pushing relentlessly on his shoulders, wanted to make himself suffer for the hell he'd brought down on Edie and Janie Tolliver.

He was miserable and he wanted to be miserable. He deserved

every last bit of misery karma could send his way, and then some.

He didn't know if that feeling would ever change.

He didn't care.

\* \* \*

Jack wasted no time upon his arrival in Newark. There was none to waste.

He was convinced, based on the lack of any background information online regarding Mike Hargus between 1987 and 2010, that the man had been an operator, probably for the CIA. But Hargus had made one critical error after leaving the agency: he'd kept his real name.

Whether because he decided secrecy was no longer necessary since he'd begun working for a legitimate political mover and shaker, or because he was simply so arrogant he believed no one would ever connect his name with a shady past, or for some other unknown reason, Mike Hargus had emerged from his nearly quarter-century-long shroud of Internet secrecy using the same name as he'd had when he entered.

Which meant that even if *he* was untraceable through normal channels for twenty-three years of his existence, his family was not. The rest of the Hargus clan had presumably not worked for the CIA, because Jack's Internet search revealed histories typical of the average American for all of them.

And there were three.

Mike Hargus had one sibling, a brother named Jimmy.

Both his parents were still alive.

All three lived in Newark.

Jimmy Hargus was two years younger than Mike and worked as a cabbie across the river in Manhattan. Tracking him down during his workday would be difficult and probably pointless, so Jack decided to hold him in reserve for now and concentrate on the retired parents. If he couldn't get what he needed from the elderly Harguses this afternoon he would stick around and hunt Jimmy down tonight.

And be as forceful as necessary.

One way or the other he wasn't leaving New Jersey without the information he needed.

# 24

Locating Bruce and Margaret Hargus was a simple matter. According to Google, they still lived in the East Newark home in which they'd raised their children decades earlier. The only real uncertainty was whether the couple would be home when Jack arrived.

They were both in their eighties, so he liked his chances.

A small, well-used Hyundai sat in front of a dilapidated garage when Jack swung into the driveway and he nodded in appreciation. Someone was here.

He wasted no time exiting his truck and approaching the house. The "reporter working on a news story" angle had worked so well for him last night that he figured he'd give it a shot again today. He arranged his features into the kind of earnest sincerity he imagined a newspaper reporter might exhibit and approached the front door, notepad in hand.

Before he could press the bell the door swung open and an elderly man scowled up at him.

"Ain't interested," the man said.

Jack raised his eyebrows. "Excuse me?"

"I said I ain't interested."

"In…"

"In whatever you're selling, or whoever you want me to vote for, or whatever municipal improvement project you're pitching. I don't care about any of it and I'm not interested, and you can just move along, thank you very much."

The old man started to swing the door closed and Jack held up his hands and slipped his foot as unobtrusively as possible between the door and the frame. The man stopped before shutting the door on Jack's foot but his scowl deepened and what little patience he had already seemed to have vanished.

Jack spoke quickly. "It's nothing like that, sir. I'm not selling anything and I honestly couldn't care less who you vote for in any election."

"Then what do you want?"

"Just a couple of minutes of your time is all. You see, my name is Ted Sanders and I'm a freelance journalist. I've been signed to do a story for The New Yorker magazine about the difficulty in protecting public figures in a dangerous world."

"Yeah? So?"

"Well I was hoping to speak with your son, Mike. As director of security for Maryland's lieutenant governor, he would make the perfect interview subject for my piece."

"So what are you doing *here*? You do realize Maryland's lieutenant governor spends most of his time in Maryland, right? Mike hasn't lived here since he was eighteen."

The old man gazed unblinkingly up at Jack. The routine that had worked so well on a young, inexperienced intern last night was going nowhere fast on the cynical old retired guy this afternoon.

"Yes, sir, I do realize that. May I please come in? I give you my word I won't take up much of your time."

"Who'd you say you work for?"

"Well, I'm a freelance journalist. I work for whoever will pay me to write, but in this case the story has been commissioned by The New Yorker."

The old guy sighed. Then he shrugged and stepped back, opening the door and gesturing reluctantly inside the house. "Come on in."

The scowl never left his face.

Jack stepped into a small but immaculate living room. The furniture had to be decades old but it was clean and well cared for. As far as he could see there wasn't a speck of dust on any surface or an item out of place anywhere in the room. A TV in the corner was tuned to a national news broadcast but the sound had been muted.

An elderly woman sat on one end of the couch. She was so tiny Jack almost missed her as he took in his surroundings.

When he noticed her he crossed the room and took her hand gently. "Hello. My name is—"

"Ted Sanders," she interrupted with an impish smile. "I heard you at the door. I'm Marge and you've already met my husband, Bruce."

Jack's immediate reaction was one of surprise. The couple struck him as so different in temperament he wondered how in the hell they'd stayed married for so long.

Bruce Hargus limped into the room and grunted something, gesturing at an overstuffed chair that had been placed at an angle opposite the couch. Jack took it as an invitation to sit and did so, opening the notebook and removing a pen from his breast pocket.

He clicked the pen and held it over the open page. "As I mentioned at the door," he said, "I'm working on a story about the difficulties inherent in protecting public figures in the modern era, and I was hoping you could help me locate your son so I could ask him a few questions for my piece."

"Bullshit," Bruce Hargus said. He'd taken a seat next to his wife on the couch and he glared at Jack defiantly.

"Bruce, please," Marge Hargus said. "Don't be rude to our guest."

"We didn't invite him here, which means he ain't our guest."

He waved at her to be quiet and continued, never taking his eyes off Jack's. "And I'll tell you something else. You ain't no reporter. I've been friends with a beat guy for the Newark Star-Ledger for thirty years, and if you're a journalist, I'm Mickey Mouse. You don't see no mouse ears around here, do ya?"

Jack clicked his pen shut.

Slipped it into his pocket.

Closed his notebook and placed it in his lap.

Tried to figure out how to proceed.

This had gone nothing like he'd expected. From the get-go this old bastard had been way ahead of him.

He had to change tactics, obviously.

He made a snap decision. What he was about to do was risky, maybe even foolish. But Bruce Hargus's voice had been filled with resentment and hurt when he'd commented at the front door that his son had not lived with them since he was eighteen.

It had not been the tone of a father proud of his son.

"You're right," Jack said. "I'm not a reporter."

"News flash," Bruce Hargus said. "No shit."

Jack lifted his wallet out of his rear pants pocket and fished around inside for a moment until he found what he was looking for. Then he removed a small, two-by-three inch photograph. It was a headshot of a smiling blonde girl. Her eyes were dancing and her nose was wrinkled as if the photographer had just said something a seven-year-old might find funny.

He placed the picture in his palm and used his right forefinger to rotate it until the smiling blonde girl was looking outward. Then he held his palm under Bruce Hargus's nose.

He never said a word.

Hargus glanced between the photo and Jack's face. The scowl was finally gone, but it had been replaced by a look of confusion.

For a long moment no one spoke. Mrs. Hargus leaned forward and craned her neck to see.

At last Bruce Hargus shrugged. "Yeah? It's a kid. So what?"

"So it's not just 'a kid.' It's my girlfriend's daughter." He wondered briefly whether the girlfriend part was still true and decided probably not.

He continued on anyway. "This little girl is named Janie and she's been kidnapped. I'd like to know—"

"Mike is not a kidnapper," Bruce Hargus snapped, his jaw jutting out aggressively.

Jack sat for a moment. He matched glares with Bruce Hargus while Marge turned sheet-white next to her husband.

"I find it interesting," Jack said, "that your initial reaction is to defend your son against a charge I never made. There are a dozen reasons I might be here that have nothing to do with Mike being a kidnapper. A hundred. Yet your gut response is to assume I believe your son took this little girl away from her mother."

Bruce Hargus's jaw snapped shut angrily but he said nothing.

"Your reaction tells me that no matter what you say, you *do* think he's capable of kidnapping this innocent child. Not only do you think he's capable of it, deep down you believe he *did* it."

The old man opened his mouth to speak, and Jack prepared to take a tongue-lashing.

But before Hargus could say a word, his wife interrupted.

"I want to speak to you in the kitchen, Bruce. *Now.*" Her voice was clipped and trembling but carried the tone of a woman who would brook no argument.

Bruce Hargus sat completely still for a heartbeat before pushing himself to his feet and limping silently out of the room. Marge followed him, ashen-faced, refusing to look at Jack.

He sat for a couple of minutes, getting antsier as time ticked away. He was tempted to follow them, if for no other reason than to satisfy himself that the old couple wasn't going to return with a couple of handguns and start blasting away. The possibility seemed ludicrously unlikely, but he'd seen stranger things in his career.

And the only thing crazier than *worrying about* getting shot by these two would be *getting* shot by these two.

He started to rise but before he could, they re-entered the living room through the door they'd exited maybe five minutes prior. Nobody was carrying a gun—except Jack, of course—and nobody started blasting away. He sank back into his chair and waited to see what would happen next.

Bruce Hargus stalked to the couch and sat in the spot his wife had previously occupied. His mouth was closed but he was clenching his jaw so tightly Jack could see the muscles corded under his weathered skin.

Mrs. Hargus took the seat closest to Jack and to his surprise, began speaking. She talked so softly he had to lean forward in his seat and concentrate hard to catch the words.

"Michael disappeared from our lives for a very long time. Initially he went into the military, some secret branch where he wasn't allowed to talk about what he was doing."

Jack listened quietly, letting the woman proceed at her own pace. Bruce sat next to her, simmering, but it was obvious he wasn't going to interrupt. At least not at the moment.

"We didn't see our son for more than twenty years," she said. "I mean, not once. Not a single Christmas or birthday, not even when Bruce suffered a stroke eight years ago."

Jack glanced at Bruce Hargus. He glared back, his face flushed and angry.

"I'm sure you can imagine how difficult that was for us," Marge continued. "Then, when he finally left the military, he started coming around again. Not a lot, but every once in a while he would show up unannounced. He'd stop in, visit for a couple of hours, and then leave and we wouldn't see him again for weeks or even months."

She sighed heavily and Jack thought she might stop talking but she didn't. Her eyes moistened and she took a moment to compose herself, but then she resumed her narrative.

"Something changed inside Michael during those twenty-odd years he was gone. He came back different. Hard. Unfeeling. He'd never been an easy child. Growing up he got into trouble, was hard to control. But now…"

She paused and Bruce Hargus leaned forward and opened his mouth to speak. She lifted her hand to shush him, exactly as he had done to her earlier, and he huffed and fumed but sat back without a word.

"Now," she continued, "Michael frightens me. His eyes are vacant. Empty. Maybe they were always that way and I just don't want to remember."

A tear rolled down her left cheek, followed immediately by one on her right. Still she kept speaking.

"You say Michael is involved in the kidnapping of that beautiful little girl. Look into your heart, Mr. Sanders, or whatever your name really is. Do you truly believe what you're saying?"

"Yes, ma'am, I do. I don't just believe it, I'm certain of it."

She nodded.

Sighed again. The sound was desolate, a stiff breeze rattling the shutters on an abandoned desert cabin.

Said, "What do you need from us, Mr. Sanders?"

"Thank you, Mrs. Hargus. I know this can't be easy."

"What do you need?"

"I need to know where your son would go if he absolutely had to keep something hidden and out of sight for a week."

"Something like a little girl."

"Yes, ma'am."

She sighed and dropped her head.

Lifted it and composed herself. "Well, I don't know. As I said,

Michael disappeared from our lives for more than two decades. And even in the years since he's been back, he shares nothing with us and we rarely see him. I honestly don't have a clue where—"

"The cabin," Bruce interrupted.

Marge Hargus fell silent and blinked.

"The cabin," she repeated, a hint of wonder in her voice. "Of course. It's been so long since we gave that thing to the boys I'd forgotten all about it."

Jack felt his pulse begin to race. "Cabin?"

Selling out his son seemed to have drained all the life from Bruce Hargus. The previously animated—if uncooperative—man closed his eyes. He rested his head on the couch back and ran a hand tiredly over his face. He suddenly looked every bit as haggard as did Mrs. Hargus.

Marge gave her husband a long look of concern before returning her attention to Jack.

"That's right," she said. "A cabin. It's been in the family for generations. Right on the water, but I'm not a water person and neither is Bruce. For that matter, neither is Michael's brother. I'm sure it's been fifteen years since Jimmy set foot inside the damned place, and it's been twice that long for us."

"I assume this cabin is secluded?"

"Oh, secluded doesn't begin to describe it. Even in the middle of the summer tourist season you feel like you're the only people on the face of the earth when you're there."

"Where's this cabin located, ma'am?"

"New Hampshire. A place called Lake Winnipesaukee."

Jack had had a lifetime's worth of experience in hiding his emotions. A blank stare and a slack expression went a long way for a man in his line of work. But he doubted he'd ever had to work as hard as he did right now to avoid showing his excitement.

Lake Winnipesaukee was less than a two-hour drive from Edie Tolliver's Southern New Hampshire neighborhood. Jack hadn't been to the lake in years, but he knew it was large, and if the cabin were as secluded as Marge Hargus claimed, it would provide a near-perfect location in which to stash a kidnap victim for a relatively short period of time.

"Can you give me the precise location of the cabin?" He

successfully kept all emotion out of his voice, but still Marge assessed him with a look that told him that for all of Bruce's bluster, *she* was the force to be reckoned with in the Hargus family.

"You're not going to the authorities with this information, are you, Mr. Sanders." She didn't phrase it as a question.

Split-second decision time again. This was an easy one. Jack had gotten nowhere inside this little ranch house until revealing the truth. He wasn't about to change course now.

"No ma'am. I'm not going to the authorities."

"You're going to try to get that little girl back on your own, aren't you?"

"Yes ma'am. And I'm going to need your help to do it."

"How so?"

"I'm counting on you not to call Michael and warn him I'm coming."

"You expect me to betray my own son? Even more than I already have? How can I do that? My desire to protect my flesh and blood is every bit as strong as your desire to protect your girlfriend's child. Probably stronger."

"I understand that, Mrs. Hargus. But if Michael knows I'm coming, he'll take Janie and disappear, and that seven-year-old child will end up at the bottom of a shallow grave. Her body will never be found. Her mother will suffer every single day for the rest of her life. You're a mother, ma'am. Try to imagine the level of pain that woman will feel."

"I don't have to imagine it. I lost my boy a long time ago." The tears flowed freely down her face now, but she held Jack's gaze steadily.

"Do you want to be the reason another mother suffers as you've suffered?"

They stared into each other's eyes, one elderly woman approaching the end of her life and one desperate man trying to save an innocent child. A child he had put in harm's way.

Bruce Hargus seemed to have checked out; his head hung on his chest and he almost appeared to be sleeping.

Marge whispered. "Please don't hurt my boy."

"I don't want to hurt anybody. All I want is to get that little girl back."

The lie passed Jack's lips easily, and even as he spoke it he wondered what that said about him.

# 25

"This ain't exactly the toughest job I've ever had to do, but it might very well be the boringest." Mike Hargus worked to keep the amusement out of his voice as he spoke into the phone. He knew how much his boss hated when he used poor grammar, which was why he tried to do exactly that as often as possible around the prissy little fucker.

Despite all he'd gained through his partnership with Bradley Chilcott—and all he yet stood to gain—he'd always resented the Maryland lieutenant governor. To Mike, Chilcott was nothing more than a pansy; a rich pretty-boy who'd benefited from all of life's advantages without ever having to get his hands dirty.

He was the opposite of Mike Hargus, in other words.

"Boring is good," Chilcott said. Mike was surprised the boss hadn't taken his bait but decided it must be because the pussy was so focused on their current operation he was barely paying attention to anything else. He was probably pissing his pants with worry.

They had agreed to touch base on the second night despite the obvious risk in doing so, just in case anything had happened on either end that might force them to amend their plan. Mike initially resisted agreeing to the phone call, but decided it was important to keep the nervous bastard reassured.

Besides, their phones were encrypted using technology similar to that employed by operational CIA case officers. The risk would be minimal.

"Things are going just fine here," he said. "Me and my partner—" he hadn't told Chilcott Byron Hunt's name and had no intention of ever doing so; it wasn't a detail the lieutenant governor needed to know—"are just sitting here with our thumbs up our asses watching one scared little kid and waiting to get back to civilization. There is literally nothing to do out here."

"Like I already said, boring is good. Sheridan still has five days to get the job done and I'm confident he'll do it. Then we'll be back on track for the White House. Just don't get antsy and do anything stupid."

*Don't do anything stupid?* Mike felt his blood pressure skyrocket. Somewhere in the back of his mind he was aware of the irony of his boss tweaking him unintentionally when Mike so loved doing it to Chilcott on purpose, but right now he was too pissed off to really give the notion the attention it deserved.

There was nothing Mike hated more than when the prissy son of a bitch talked down to him. *He* was the one with his ass hanging out doing all the heavy lifting and taking all the chances, while Mr. Bigshot Lieutenant Governor sat down there in his cushy mansion drinking too much and second-guessing everything. Fucking sanctimonious little asshole.

Mike took a deep breath in an attempt to calm himself.

It mostly didn't work.

He said, "Listen, college boy, don't you worry about me. I was running covert ops in Afghanistan while the girls in junior high were beating you up for your lunch money. I'll be fine. I've done jobs like this a dozen times and I'm not worried about holding up my end. You wanna know what *does* worry me?"

Silence. Chilcott was either too surprised by Mike's reaction to answer or too angry.

Either way, Mike considered it a win and he continued. "I'm worried about *you*. You just try to keep your dick in your pants and not get caught roughing up any hookers or, God forbid, high school girls. I can't clean up your messes while I'm stuck out here in the middle of nowhere, babysitting a seven-year-old."

"Don't you talk to me in that tone of voice. Remember who signs your paycheck every two weeks. I expect a certain level of respect out of my employees."

"Is that so? Well don't *you* forget who knows where all the bodies are buried. Literally. We stopped being employer and employee a long time ago. We're partners now, *sir*. I'll show deference in public but at moments like this we're equals right down the line. You'd do well to remember that."

More silence on the other end of the line. Bradley Chilcott's shock and fury at this mutiny couldn't have been more obvious, and once again Mike had to work to suppress a chuckle. God, he loved fucking with the big pussy.

After maybe ten seconds, Chilcott answered. His voice was cold and hard and a little shaky. "Just keep an eye on the girl. This will all be over in a few days."

The line went dead and this time Mike laughed out loud.

\* \* \*

Bradley slammed his cell phone down so hard it made the photographs of his wife and kids skitter nervously toward the edge of his desk. He couldn't remember the last time he'd been this angry.

Stress probably had something to do with it, but still, to be treated so rudely by a man who didn't even have the sense to recognize Bradley's place in the pecking order was galling.

It was also cause for concern.

Mike Hargus had always been difficult to control. He was a hard man, and dangerous, which was exactly what made him so valuable to someone like Bradley Chilcott.

But his value evaporated the moment he became a threat.

And his statement—that he knew where all the bodies were buried—was not only accurate it was dangerous. Bradley wasn't stupid, he knew full well Hargus resented him and enjoyed nothing more than needling him.

But this time the man had crossed a line. This time he'd issued a direct challenge to Bradley's authority, and that was something Bradley Chilcott could not let stand.

Mike Hargus was not Bradley's equal. He would never *be* Bradley's equal. He had clearly forgotten his place in the grand scheme of things.

It was time to consider cutting Hargus loose. Of course, firing him would be out of the question. Hargus would never take something like a dismissal lying down. He would hit back hard, and in so doing could demolish Bradley's career like a stick of dynamite blowing up a house of cards.

There was only one reasonable option.

Mike Hargus would have to be eliminated.

Permanently.

Because he was right about one thing: he *did* know where the bodies were buried. Most of them, anyway.

But what he didn't know—or didn't seem to appreciate—was that while Bradley's intelligence community connections were growing colder the longer he sat in the Maryland State House, for the moment at least they remained viable.

The same connections that had been mined to recruit Mike Hargus from the CIA six years ago could be mined again and used to recruit another director of security, one who wouldn't represent the potential for personal and professional ruin. One without Hargus's goddamned independent streak.

Bradley leaned back and stared off into space as he considered the disturbing phone call he'd just taken. He had hoped to feel better after talking to Hargus but instead he felt immeasurably worse.

More threatened.

Much more worried.

Kim knocked on his office door and he ignored it. Her muffled voice floated through the heavy oak telling him dinner was ready and he ignored that, too.

Obviously he could take no action against Hargus until this operation was over, and that was fine. He wasn't ready to proceed with the man's elimination yet, anyway.

But in five days or less, Jim Studds would be dead and Mike Hargus would become a liability. A loose thread that would have to be snipped.

Bradley leaned back in his chair and lifted his feet onto his desktop. Kim had finally gotten the message that Bradley didn't want to be disturbed and had stopped banging on the door.

Getting rid of Hargus would require some scheming. The last

thing Bradley wanted was to go about it the wrong way, to act rashly and end up in exactly the same situation with someone else that he was currently in with his director of security.

But scheming was what he did. It was his dominant trait and he was certain that if he gave the issue the attention it deserved he would come up with a workable solution.

Maybe there was even a way to get Jack Sheridan to eliminate Hargus. That would be as fitting as it was ironic.

Bradley nodded, all alone in his office. He had some serious thinking to do.

# 26

The first thing Jack noticed about the cottage was that the blinds on all the windows visible from his location had been drawn tightly. A car was parked in the dirt driveway, and even though it was tagged with New Hampshire plates, Jack took its presence as a very good sign. The kidnapper wouldn't have used his own car, so this one was obviously stolen.

He hadn't been convinced Marge Hargus wouldn't change her mind and warn her son that Jack was coming for him. He'd given the subject a lot of thought on the drive north from New Jersey and placed the odds at roughly fifty-fifty. But if she'd contacted him, Hargus and Janie would have been long gone and the cottage abandoned by the time he arrived.

And someone was in there.

He'd driven straight to Lake Winnipesaukee after leaving Newark. The route to the lake would take him straight past the I-93 exit for his home, and the urge to stop and check in on Edie was almost overwhelming. But he forced himself to maintain his speed and continue past the exit. He simply could not afford to sacrifice the time it would take to stop at his house.

He planned his arrival at Winnipesaukee for the dead of night, which came with obvious advantages but also considerable risk. Jack would be approaching a home he'd never seen that was located in an area he'd never visited. The cottage was isolated, which meant his presence would stick out like a sore thumb were he to be spotted by Hargus.

GPS navigation simplified the process of locating the cabin, but for a short while Jack feared he'd been snookered by Marge Hargus and sent on a wild goose chase. The road providing access to the cottage was narrow and winding, filled with potholes and bordered on both sides by thickly forested wilderness. Residences were few and far between, and the ones Jack passed all looked empty—summer homes whose owners had not yet opened them for the season.

No wonder Hargus had chosen this area to stash Janie.

When the GPS informed him he was roughly a quarter-mile from his destination he killed the headlights and inched forward, his truck's engine growling softly, almost but not quite at idle power.

Five hundred feet from the cottage he pulled as far to the side of the road as he could and shut down. The rest of the way he would travel on foot. He would have to return for his supplies and to hide the truck, but based on the lack of activity he'd observed as well as the time—it was now well past midnight—he felt comfortable leaving it exposed for the time being.

In the unlikely event someone came by and the even *more* unlikely event that person became suspicious and stopped, Jack would simply feign a breakdown. He'd done it before and it always worked when accompanied by a gruff demeanor and an open engine compartment.

He lifted the truck's hood and then hiked the rest of the way to the cabin, melting into the woods on the opposite side of the narrow access road when it came into view. Then he searched until finding a satisfactory surveillance location: one that would provide unobstructed sightlines for as much of the home as possible but which would also minimize the chances of him being seen by the occupants.

He settled in and slipped on his night vision goggles. For more than three hours he kept watch, expecting no activity and seeing none. The cottage was small and Jack guessed its interior featured a combination kitchen/living area, a bathroom and probably two tiny bedrooms, one of which undoubtedly held Janie Tolliver.

A light shone through the blinds covering one of the windows. That would be the kitchen/living area. Jack wondered whether

Hargus was alone or if he'd recruited a conspirator. He guessed, based on Hargus's history as an operator, that there was one other person inside the cabin besides Janie and Hargus. Even though their captive was a little girl and essentially harmless, Hargus would want to maintain a round-the-clock watch in order to stave off any potential difficulties that might arise while asleep.

It's not how Jack would have handled things, but Jack was a loner. He always had been.

At four a.m. he returned to his truck. Not a single car had driven past on the access road during the three hours he'd been monitoring the kidnappers' hideaway, but Jack wasn't prepared to assume the situation wouldn't change in the morning.

Locating an appropriate-sized opening between the massive trees took some time. The forest was thick and ancient and overgrown with towering Douglas firs as well as smaller but still significant oaks and cedars. Jack started searching at the spot he'd parked the truck, moving slowly away from the cottage.

Eventually he found the gap he was looking for.

He returned to his truck and lowered the hood. Then he started it up and reversed along the road, backing tailgate-first into the area he'd selected. He killed the engine and then screened the opening between the truck and the road as effectively as possible in the darkness and without a saw to cut branches. He worked quickly, straightening and restoring the underbrush that had been crushed beneath the truck's wheels.

The results seemed acceptable if not perfect. From the road, Jack thought it was unlikely the Ram would be seen by anyone not specifically searching for it.

The sun began insinuating itself into the sky a little after five a.m., but by that time Jack had removed his backpack from the truck and returned to his surveillance location directly across the pockmarked road from the kidnappers' cottage.

The rest of the day he spent watching.

Planning.

Preparing.

\* \* \*

The time passed slowly, but that was fine with Jack. He needed as much prep time for his assault as he could reasonably manage without further endangering Janie.

Taking on an experienced operator would be difficult enough, even with the advantage of surprise on his side. Hargus was on his own turf and knew the area; Jack was in unfamiliar territory and did not. Hargus was ensconced in an easily defensible structure; Jack would have to cross at least sixty feet of open ground just to make his approach.

This would not be easy.

Jack didn't care.

\* \* \*

Around midday a man stepped out the cottage's only door. He walked onto the back deck and flipped a cigarette butt into the water that lapped right up against the massive granite boulders serving as the cottage's foundation. He stretched and yawned and Jack took the opportunity to study him.

He was a white man, and he was large, with the look of an athlete long gone to seed: big in the arms and shoulders, with thick hips and a gut that hung over his belt. Jack guessed his belly was expanding a little more with each passing year.

The man leaned on the deck's railing and stared uninterestedly at the empty expanse of water before yawning a second time—apparently keeping watch over a seven-year-old was tiring work—and slouching back inside. He slammed the door behind him and the cottage fell still again.

A couple of hours later the door opened again and a second man repeated the process, duplicating the first man's actions almost precisely. This man was black, taller than the white kidnapper but slim and wiry. He moved with the quick, herky-jerky motions of a speed freak and Jack made a mental note that when the time came, he would have to put this guy down hard to ensure he stayed down.

The first man out of the cottage had obviously been Hargus.

The second must be whomever Hargus had hired—undoubtedly another operator—to help share the workload over the seven-day period while they hid Janie away and awaited the news of Maryland Governor Jim Studds' assassination.

No one else came or left the cottage over the course of the day. Jack doubted a third man was inside. Two would be plenty—more than plenty, really—to prevent the escape of a child from a secure location, and adding more people to the conspiracy would only make maintaining secrecy upon the job's completion that much more difficult.

It would be hard enough to do with a pair of conspirators, and Jack wondered whether it had occurred to the nameless second operator that he might just become expendable once the job was over.

He didn't waste much time worrying about it.

The sun was starting to set when Jack rose to his feet and slipped further back into the trees. He'd nibbled on energy bars over the course of the day and made sure to stay hydrated by drinking water, and he felt strong and fresh. He'd been on plenty of stakeouts that had lasted a lot longer than sixteen hours, and under much more difficult conditions.

When he felt he'd put sufficient distance between himself and the cottage to prevent the kidnappers from overhearing, he removed his cell phone and pressed the auto-dial for Edie's cell. He'd been concerned about a lack of cell coverage when he learned the location of the hideaway, but his worries had been baseless. The signal was strong. There was a cell tower somewhere close by, probably thanks to Winnipesaukee's status as a popular vacation destination.

Jack was unsurprised when his call was answered almost immediately. He pictured Edie pacing his small living room, alone and terrified, and hated himself just a little more for what he'd done to her.

"Hello? Jack? Do you have Janie? Have you seen her? Is she okay?"

"Easy, Edie. Slow down. No, I haven't seen Janie specifically but I'm one hundred percent certain she's okay. Remember, they need her alive and unharmed or they lose their leverage over me."

"I know. The waiting is just so hard."

"I understand. It won't be long now, I promise."

"Okay."

"Have you heard from Janie yesterday and today?"

"Yes. I started to get worried that she wasn't going to call but she did, at about the same time both days. Around midafternoon. I barely got to speak with her each time but it was definitely her. She sounded scared but okay. She said she was bored and asked when she could come home."

"That's good. If her major complaint is boredom, it's obvious she's not being mistreated."

"Other than being ripped from her mother's arms and taken hostage in an assassination plot."

"Other than that." Jack felt his face redden with shame despite being alone in the woods. "Hang in there, Edie. She's a tough kid, and she'll be back with you very soon."

"When are you going to get her? How much longer do I have to wait?"

Jack hesitated. Edie was suffering under a tremendous strain. It was obvious based just on this phone call that she was barely keeping herself together. If he told her he would have her little girl back in her arms by tomorrow and then didn't deliver, he worried it might be more than she could handle.

Edie picked up on his hesitation and jumped on it. "What is it, Jack? What are you not telling me? Is something wrong?"

"No, nothing's wrong. I was trying to decide how to answer your question, that's all."

"And?"

"And I promise I'll have her back to you absolutely as fast as I can manage. But the most important consideration is Janie's safety, so it's critical I take my time and do this right. I'm only going to get one chance and I have to make it count."

"Jack, they…they asked to speak with you when they called."

"Both times?"

"No, just the second time. This afternoon."

"And what did you tell them?"

"I said exactly what you told me to. I said you were off some-where working on their assignment. I told them I didn't know where you'd gone or when you would be back because you refused to tell me."

"Perfect. You did great."

Silence fell over the line and stretched on.

At last Edie broke it. "You'll call again tomorrow, right?"

"Of course. I'll call every day until I have Janie back to you, and that's a promise."

More silence.

"You know what you're doing, right Jack? Please tell me you know what you're doing."

"Yes, Edie, I know what I'm doing. God help me, but I know what I'm doing."

# 27

Dusk seemed to linger forever. The cottage began to fade from view as Jack resumed surveillance, its structural details losing definition with the disappearance of the sun. Eventually the building was swallowed up by the darkness but for the single light shining from behind the blinds covering the largest window.

As long as it had taken for the late-spring night to fall in northern New Hampshire, the appearance of the stars in the cloudless sky afterward seemed to occur almost instantly. And they were dazzling. With the absence of artificial illumination, the natural light show overhead was breathtaking.

Jack barely noticed. All of his attention was devoted to the mission, his focus entirely on the kidnappers of Janie Tolliver.

The temperature began to drop and Jack barely noticed that, too. Even though it was almost June, nighttime temperatures in this area routinely approached freezing, but he was prepared for that and more.

After completing his call to Edie, he'd unzipped his equipment bag and changed into layered survival gear from head to toe. The temperature could plummet all the way to zero degrees Fahrenheit before he would begin to feel a chill seeping through his clothing.

Even if that happened he would endure it if necessary. He'd gone through much worse to complete missions that meant far less to him.

Jack sat quietly, NVE over his head, watching the cottage and scanning the surrounding area. Neither kidnapper had reappeared since their separate treks onto the deck this afternoon. No one had come or gone. Were it not for the car parked in the gravel driveway and the ever-present dim light shining in the one window there would be no indication anyone was even inside.

But they *were* inside. Jack's initial surveillance had revealed that the structure contained only one entrance. With the exception of his five-minute phone call to Edie, when he'd backtracked into the forest to avoid detection, he hadn't taken his eyes off that door in better than twenty-four hours. Unless Mike Hargus and his anonymous co-conspirator had climbed out a rear window and rowed a boat across Lake Winnipesaukee, they were inside that cottage.

He forced himself to maintain concentration. Craved coffee but didn't want to become jittery. Janie's life might well come down to a single well-placed shot, and Jack wasn't about to jeopardize an innocent girl's life to satisfy his caffeine addiction.

Because he had already decided he would make his move tonight.

He'd learned all he could through surveillance, and watching the cottage another day would gain him nothing of value. But although the night was already as dark as it would get, Jack forced himself to wait a few more hours. Anyone familiar with the techniques and tactics of guerilla warfare knew the best time to execute a nocturnal assault was between the hours of three and four in the morning, when natural human biorhythms were at their ebb.

Jack was familiar with those techniques and tactics. They'd kept him alive in the past and he was counting on them to do so again tonight.

So he waited. Conditions were generally favorable for what he had planned with one exception: the moon was nearly full. With almost no clouds to provide cover, the moon and stars combined to throw far more light than Jack would have preferred.

If Hargus or his buddy picked the wrong moment to glance out a window, Jack's advantage of surprise would disappear in an instant and he would likely find himself face-down and bleeding out before he ever got within twenty feet of the kidnappers' hideaway.

There was nothing he could do about the lack of cloud cover, so he disregarded it. He would make up for the less-than-optimal lighting by exercising extra caution.

Or he would die.

Worrying about it would change nothing.

\* \* \*

Three a.m. came and went. Jack was in no danger of falling asleep despite the fact he'd been awake almost continuously for close to forty-four hours. Adrenaline buzzed through his body and he was thankful he'd foregone the coffee he considered drinking earlier.

He pushed to his feet, conscious of his cracking knees and stiff back. His body served to remind him—as if he stood any chance of forgetting—that he was ancient by operator standards although not even middle age by normal measures.

He warmed up, soundlessly running in place, doing a half-dozen squats and then dropping to a prone position and whipping off a quick dozen pushups. In less than a minute he'd generated a thin sheen of perspiration and gotten his blood pumping again. His joints felt loose—more or less—and he decided he was ready to proceed.

He pulled a pair of latex gloves out of his pocket and slipped them on. Then he started walking, moving straight through the trees, concerned more about being heard than seen. There was no way the sentry across the road could be using night vision equipment. The light burning inside the cottage would render him effectively blind if that were the case.

However, it was certainly possible a window had been left cracked for airflow, and in the funereal silence of the Lake Winnipesauke shoreline, a cracking branch would sound almost as loud as a gunshot to anyone paying attention.

Jack took his time, picking his way around and over obstacles, finally reaching the side of the narrow road at a point approximately seventy feet northwest of the cottage, on the side of the house farthest away from the window with the light on. He crossed the road, not quite sprinting but moving quickly, and then began working back toward the cottage.

By three-thirty he'd arrived at a point almost directly across from where he'd been conducting surveillance for the last day-and-a-half. He flattened himself against the trunk of an ancient oak tree and caught his breath.

Planned his next move.

Prepared to recover Janie.

He lifted his Sig out of its holster and chambered a round. Then he crossed the open side yard, keeping the kidnappers' vehicle between himself and the cottage. Ducking behind the car, Jack took two deep, calming breaths and then continued moving.

Seconds later he'd flattened himself against the side wall next to a closed window. The blinds were drawn—of course—and Jack wondered if Janie was just inches away, huddled on the other side of the wall, afraid and alone.

*Hang in there, kid.*

He slowed his breathing and listened for anything that might give him some idea of Hargus's location, or of the wiry black speed freak the operator had brought in to keep him company. A conversation, or a radio turned down low, or a cough or the flush of a toilet or maybe the scrape of a chair on the floor.

But there was nothing.

He began moving again, sidling toward the rear of the home and the lakeshore he could hear lapping against the granite boulders.

A second window indicated the presence of either a second bedroom or possibly the bathroom. The blinds were drawn and this window was as dark as the previous one had been. Jack repeated the procedure he'd just attempted, slowing his breathing and listening intently, but was rewarded with the same disappointing result: absolutely nothing.

He shook his head and continued.

He rounded the cottage's southwest corner and climbed onto the boulder. Then he lifted himself over the deck railing and dropped soundlessly to the other side. It only took one small step to convince Jack he would have to use extreme caution. The deck boards felt soft and spongy underfoot.

He inched toward a massive picture window that offered what was likely a breathtaking view of Lake Winnipesaukee and the surrounding wilderness. But Jack wasn't interested in the view.

He crept to the corner of the picture window. It was old, had likely been installed sixty or seventy years ago, and consisted of one large pane of thick glass flanked on each side by a traditional double-hung window. The configuration would permit the resident to lift the windows on either side to allow cooling lake air into the cottage, while still permitting blinds to be drawn over the picture window when the sun's rays were beating down on that side of the cottage.

It was a sensible configuration.

It was also the source of Jack's first break.

Because the double-hung window closest to Jack was cracked open—not much, only a couple of inches, but the kidnappers had obviously felt safe unlocking a rear window in order to remove some of the stuffiness from a structure that had probably not been inhabited in quite some time.

To allow the air inside they'd had to lift the blinds. Again, not all the way. Only a couple of inches. Most of the window was still covered.

But two inches was all Jack needed.

He bent and peered through the narrow slit into the cottage.

As he'd suspected, this portion of the interior was a combination kitchen/living area. A low wattage bulb burned inside a table lamp that was probably old enough to be an antique. The lamp sat atop a scarred kitchen table placed directly in the center of the room.

A ratty couch ran along the wall just below the window through which Jack peered, and a gas cookstove that had to be older than Jack sat in the corner next to an equally ancient refrigerator. A couple of bags of groceries had been thrown haphazardly onto a chipped Formica counter. One of the bags had tipped onto its side, and a jar of spaghetti sauce had tumbled out next to a carton of cigarettes.

A case of cheap canned beer had been dropped onto the floor next to the doorway, which was off to Jack's right. The kidnappers had worked steadily through the beer and now maybe eight cans remained unopened. The empties had been tossed haphazardly around the living area.

The pungent scent of cigar smoke wafted through the open window and Jack shook his head scornfully. These guys were so overconfident they were treating a felony kidnapping—not to mention conspiracy to commit murder—like the weekend at a frat house.

Seated at the kitchen table was the wiry black man Jack had seen outside the cottage earlier in the day. The speed freak. A deck of cards and a handgun lay on the table in front of him and he sat in an uncomfortable-looking wooden chair with his head back, eyes closed, softly snoring.

There was no sign of Mike Hargus. Presumably he was sleeping in one of the bedrooms behind the pair of closed doors to Jack's left, with Janie restrained behind the other.

Jack watched for several minutes as the kidnapper slept on. Then he ducked away from the window and got to work.

# 28

Jack crouched on the deck below and just to the side of the open window.

Reached into his jacket pocket and removed a Sig Sauer SRD9 titanium sound suppressor.

Threaded it onto the muzzle of his pistol, working with practiced efficiency.

Then he placed the gun on the deck beside his knees—readily accessible should his situation change rapidly—and pulled a utility knife from his other pocket. The knife featured a razor-sharp blade, extendible via a thumb switch.

He deployed the blade and eased his eyes over the window sash. Inside, the kidnapper snored on, head still tilted back and against his right shoulder. Nothing appeared to have changed inside the cabin.

Still no sign of Janie or Hargus.

Jack reached up and began sawing through the screen, working quickly but quietly with a compact cutting motion. He sliced the mesh at its outer edges, where it attached to the aluminum frame, which he supported with his left hand to minimize noise. In less than two minutes the screen lay on the deck planking and all that stood between Jack and the cottage's interior was the partially open window.

He picked up his now-silenced Sig and rechecked the interior of the cottage.

No change.

He reached under the window and pushed it up on its tracks slowly, prepared to go to Plan B the moment he heard any screeching or squeaking. But noise was minimal and was covered nicely by the sentry's snores. In seconds Jack had pushed it as high as it would go.

He now had a means of entry into the cottage.

And still the sentry slept.

Jack supported his Sig against his right hip, aiming it inside the cottage—not directly it at the sentry, but close enough—as he sat on the window frame. He ducked under the window he'd raised and then pivoted, swinging his feet into the kitchen/living area. He slipped to the floor and was in.

The "plan"—although calling it a plan was probably doing a grave disservice to the term—was to cross the room and place his gun against the sentry's head. Jack would then wake the man and force him to reveal which bedroom contained Janie and which contained Hargus.

Then he would secure Hargus and recover Janie.

Simple. Also risky.

He'd taken two steps, covered roughly one-third of the distance between the window and the sleeping man, when without warning the sentry straightened his head and opened his eyes. The man stared at Jack for a half-second, his mouth hanging open in shock, as if he couldn't quite convince himself he wasn't dreaming.

Then he reached for his gun with a lightning-quick motion.

Jack squeezed off a shot. The silenced slug ripped into the man's shoulder, knocking him off his chair and onto the floor with a heavy thud.

*Dammit. That was too much noise.*

He stepped forward and grabbed the sentry's weapon. Shoved it into the waistband of his trousers at the small of his back as the sentry writhed in pain on the floor.

Then he spun to face the closed bedroom doors but it was too late.

One was no longer closed.

In the doorway stood Mike Hargus. He'd positioned himself directly behind the sleepy, terrified Janie Tolliver and he held the barrel of his gun flush against the side of her head.

How he'd gotten into this defensive position so quickly Jack had no idea.

Maybe Hargus had seen Jack approaching the cottage.

Maybe he'd rigged some kind of rudimentary alarm system to the windows. Jack hadn't noticed one but that didn't mean much.

How he'd managed it didn't matter at this point. Things had gone sideways in near-record time and now Jack's only advantage—surprise—was gone.

"Funny," Hargus said. "I don't see Jim Studds in this room. You should be hundreds of miles away from here completing your assignment." His voice was cold and hard.

Jack ignored him and focused on Janie. Her eyes were fearful, darting between Jack and the bleeding sentry, who continued to thrash on the floor in pain. He was afraid in her panic she might try to wrench out of her captor's grasp and catch a bullet in the back.

"It's okay, Janie," he said softly. He removed his left hand from the gun and made a *calm down* motion. "Everything's going to be fine."

Hargus snickered. "Not a big believer in the power of honesty, are you, Sheridan?"

Jack said nothing but shifted his attention to Hargus. Gauged the odds of shooting the man as he stood behind Janie using her small form as a human shield.

Hargus was much bigger than the frightened seven-year-old and Jack was an excellent marksman. He guessed if he took the shot one hundred times from this distance and under these circumstances he would bury a slug in Hargus's forehead at least ninety-five of them.

But a ninety-five percent chance of success wasn't good enough.

And even if he were to shoot Hargus dead, there was always the possibility—the likelihood, really—that the man would squeeze the trigger of his own gun reflexively as he fell. Given the fact it was pressed against Janie's skull, *she* would be dead before *he* hit the ground.

Hargus watched Jack go through his calculations, a grim half-smile on his face. Then he shook his head. "Bad plan," he said. "It won't work."

Jack realized the man was following his train of thought exactly. He cursed to himself. He might as well be thinking out loud, announcing his intentions to the ex-operator.

If he didn't begin thinking outside the box—right now, at this exact moment—the standoff would turn into a bloodbath and Janie would die.

"Lower your gun. Do it now," Hargus said. His voice had become raspy and aggressive as he sought to gain control of the situation.

Jack shook his head without speaking.

"Transfer your gun to your left hand," Hargus continued. "Then place it on the kitchen table and step away from it."

"Not going to happen," Jack said.

"It *is* gonna happen. Because if you don't do as I say, and right this fucking minute, this little brat catches a bullet in the brain pan."

"I don't think so."

"Are you out of your fucking mind? You don't think I can shoot a kid? You're playing with fire, asshole, and you're about to get burned."

"Oh, I don't doubt you could shoot a child. You've already proven you're capable of anything. But you're not going to do it, because the moment you pull that trigger you have nothing left to hide your worthless ass behind. Shoot her and half a second later you'll be the recipient of two 9mm slugs to your own skull. You might be a murderous, amoral, opportunistic thug, but you're not about to sacrifice your life for the likes of Bradley Chilcott."

Hargus grinned. "You're right about that one. But we've got a bit of a problem, then, don't we? If I shoot the girl, I die. If you shoot me, the girl dies. Perfect standoff."

Hargus continued to show no sign of nerves or fear. The man's ability to maintain his cool under tremendous pressure was the unmistakable sign of a professional operator who'd been well trained and who had honed his skills over years of dangerous missions.

*Think outside the box.*

Hargus was an operator.

He'd received training similar to Jack's.

He would react in certain predictable ways to threat situations. *Use that knowledge to your advantage.*

An operator was taught always to deal with the source of an immediate threat first, before all else. Eliminate the threat and then move on.

And just like that, Jack knew what he had to do. The plan of attack arrived fully formed and ready for implementation, the product of a lifetime's experience.

If he executed it properly, he might yet save Janie's life, not to mention his own.

If he didn't, they would both almost certainly die.

Hargus was still speaking. He was trying to distract Jack, waiting for an opening in which to make his own move.

Jack ignored him, desperately considering any possible options beyond the one he already knew he would have to use.

There were none.

Hargus was saying something about it not being too late for Jack to walk back out the door and go kill Jim Studds, that they could forget any of this had ever happened. It was a lie he had to know Jack would recognize immediately. But he continued to push the point.

Jack held his eyes for a moment. Then he shifted the barrel of his Sig slightly and fired one slug into the lamp on the kitchen table.

Instantly the room was plunged into darkness.

# 29

Jack was risking everything on Hargus operating instinctively and falling back on his training. He would *deal with the source of the immediate threat first*, lifting his gun and firing at Jack rather than pumping a bullet into Janie Tolliver's brain.

Jack was moving even before his silenced weapon spit out the slug and shattered the lamp. The light vanished and a split-second's shocked silence dropped over the room, and then everything happened at once.

Janie screamed and Hargus cursed and Jack dived to the right. He was counting on Hargus firing instinctively at the spot where Jack had been standing when he shot out the table lamp.

But by then he would be somewhere else.

Jack hit the floor and smashed into the wall with a bone-jarring crash. His shoulder struck first, followed instantly by the side of his head. The force of the impact jarred his gun loose and he heard it skitter away and bounce off the wall.

Hargus's weapon boomed, the percussive sound almost unbearably loud inside the small, enclosed space of the cottage. Instantly Janie's screams took on a muffled, underwater tone.

The location of the muzzle flash told Jack his gamble had paid off. Hargus was dealing with the source of the immediate threat, firing at Jack rather than Janie. But he would recover quickly, and Jack's desperate gamble could still turn tragic in a heartbeat.

Pain ripped through his shoulder and head, dual lightning bolts that he ignored. His arms and legs scrabbled for purchase and he pushed himself to a half-standing position even as he registered the fact that he no longer held his gun.

Then he launched himself at Mike Hargus. The muzzle flash had shown him exactly where to aim his tackle, even with his vision still blurry and his skull pounding from the collision with the wall.

Hargus squeezed the trigger a second time, adjusting to the changing situation quickly, shifting his aim to the left and firing at Jack. A second ear-splitting BOOM shook the house and a second muzzle flash verified that Janie Tolliver was still standing, still very much alive.

The slug whizzed past Jack's ear just as he crashed into the kidnapper and his little victim. Janie's voice broke off in mid-scream and the force of the impact sent her flying backward. She tumbled into the same wall Jack had just bounced off and then crumpled to the floor.

In the back of his mind Jack hoped he hadn't hurt her too badly but there was nothing he could do about it now.

He continued to drive with his legs, his injured shoulder buried in Mike Hargus's midsection, and a half-second later they smashed into the cookstove. It was where the sentry had dragged himself after being shot and he screamed in pain as Jack and Hargus fell on top of him in a tangle of arms and legs.

The impact with the stove twisted them sideways and Hargus landed on top. Jack reached for the sentry's gun, the one he'd jammed into the waistband of his pants, but it was gone. Apparently it too had been shaken loose by the same violent encounter with the wall that had caused him to drop his own weapon.

*Dammit.*

He cringed as he adjusted on the fly, moving to Plan C, waiting to feel Mike Hargus's bullets ripping into his body and dropping the curtain on this shit show for good.

But there was no more gunfire. Hargus must have lost his grip on his own weapon when Jack tackled him. Instead of shooting, the kidnapper pounded a fist into the side of Jack's skull, rocking him and causing a flash of light that he dimly realized was exploding inside his own head.

He shook off the blow and returned a punch, a jab launched

somewhere in the direction of Hargus's face with his left hand as he fumbled in his jacket pocket with his right.

Hargus struck again, another blow to nearly the same spot, and Jack's head bounced off the corner of the cookstove and the same light he'd seen before flashed again and he was bleeding, he could feel the blood rolling down the side of his head and he knew he was about to be overwhelmed by the much bigger Hargus. A couple more punches would short-circuit his brain and by the time he could recover it would be too late.

The fingers of his right hand closed around the item he was looking for in his pocket as Hargus hit him again, and he thumbed the utility knife open as he yanked it from his pocket, and Hargus hit him a fourth time just as Jack slashed upward with the blade, aiming for where he guessed Hargus's throat to be.

He struck hard and hit resistance, the knife digging into soft skin before scraping sideways along bone. Hargus gasped, a quick intake of breath as he reacted to being slashed, and then grunted in pain and shock as blood soaked Jack's hand, a tidal wave that was warm and wet and told Jack he'd struck paydirt: the kidnapper's jugular.

The punches stopped coming. Hargus slapped both hands to his neck in an attempt to stanch the heavy bleeding. He coughed and gurgled and blood sprayed. He thrashed his legs violently, exactly as the sentry had done when Jack shot him.

Hargus was trying to speak as Jack shoved the bigger man off him and staggered to his feet. Blood continued to flow sluggishly down the side of his own head, starting somewhere under his hairline, running down his jaw and dripping to the floor. He could already feel his face beginning to swell from Mike Hargus's heavy fists.

Hargus continued to try to speak and he continued to be unsuccessful.

Jack continued to ignore him in any event. Even with his ears ringing from the punches he'd taken in the head and the pair of close-quarters gunshots Hargus had fired, Jack knew he should be able to hear Janie screaming or crying.

And he couldn't.

He couldn't hear anything besides Mike Hargus's steadily

weakening attempts to speak with his throat sliced open, to make Jack aware how badly he'd been hurt and that he needed help, as if maybe Jack didn't know.

Jack still ignored him. He ignored everything but the cold, sick feeling in the pit of his stomach, the one that told him the bullet he'd felt whiz past his ear had ricocheted, had bounced off something inside the cottage and struck Janie, and that even now she lay dead or dying.

He fumbled for his phone, praying it hadn't been broken or damaged in the fight with Hargus. Lifted it out of his pocket and activated the flashlight app. Shined it with shaking hands around the inside of the cottage until his eyes fell on Janie's small body.

She was crumpled on the floor at the base of the wall, next to the door Hargus had stepped through while using her as a human shield. Her legs were drawn up to her chest and she lay on her side in the fetal position.

Her eyes were closed.

She wasn't moving.

Jack pivoted quickly, illuminating the prone bodies of Hargus and his co-conspirator. As desperate as he was to check on Janie, he had to ensure neither man was a threat. He would be useless to Janie if one of the kidnappers were to clock him over the head while he was tending to her.

The sentry Jack had shot was struggling to extricate himself from beneath Hargus, whose injury looked even more severe in the light than Jack had guessed. Bradley Chilcott's Chief of Security was bleeding all over the man pinned beneath him, a crimson arterial flow that poured out around and through the fingers of both hands, which were pressed tightly to his neck.

Hargus's legs continued to piston, but he was losing strength rapidly and his eyes were beginning to glaze over.

It was clear that without prompt and professional medical attention Hargus would not survive. His injuries were too severe, the blood loss too complete. Even had a fully stocked ambulance been standing by, Jack doubted it would make any difference.

He couldn't bring himself to muster any sympathy for the dying man.

The second man looked as though he would probably survive,

although he would clearly not present a threat. *His* hands were pressed tightly against the bullet wound in his shoulder and he was in obvious pain. And he was still trapped under Mike Hargus.

Jack turned back toward Janie.

She still hadn't moved.

He hurried to her and knelt, fearing the worst.

# 30

Janie didn't seem to be bleeding. It was impossible to be sure given the poor lighting, but Jack examined her as closely as he could without moving her and he couldn't find any indication she'd been shot.

The cold ball of fear in the pit of his stomach dissipated slightly.

He ran his fingers over her skull, starting at her forehead and moving into her hairline on each side until his fingers met in back. If she hadn't been shot, she was likely unconscious because she'd struck her head against the wall when Jack tackled Hargus. The collision had been violent and Janie was small for her age.

A growing goose egg on the back of Janie's head confirmed Jack's suspicions and he began to breathe a little easier. Losing consciousness was never a good thing, and a concussion was a very real possibility, but she would survive.

Jack eased Janie's head to the floor and stood. He hated to leave her where she was, but it would only be for a little longer. Then he could get her the hell out of this house of horrors and back to her mother where she belonged.

The moment he returned his attention to Hargus he knew the man was gone. The blood that had been gushing from his neck just moments ago had now almost completely stopped. His eyes were open but they stared lifelessly forward.

The other man had somehow succeeded in wriggling the upper portion of his body out from under his dead partner, but without assistance he would never manage the rest. He looked up at Jack, his eyes pleading.

"Help me," he whispered. "I don't want to die trapped under a corpse."

"Maybe you should have considered that possibility before you threw in with a scumbag like Mike Hargus."

"Listen," the man said. "I didn't have a fucking clue what Hargus was up to. None of this has a damned thing to do with me. He called me and asked if I was interested in making a quick five grand babysitting a little kid for a week. Of course I said yes."

"Of course you did. Don't even try to convince me you didn't know this poor little girl had been kidnapped."

"Listen, man, I'm not in any position to try to bullshit you, I realize that. You hold all the cards and I understand I'm at your mercy. So I'm laying it all on the line. Sure, I knew the kid had been taken. But Hargus swore nobody was gonna get hurt. He told me he was in position to make a big-time score but that the kid would be released after a week unharmed no matter what happened."

Jack gazed down at the injured man appraisingly. Probably most of what he said was true, although Jack doubted it had made the slightest bit of difference to this guy whether the kidnapping victim was ultimately released unharmed or not. Since they'd not taken any measures to prevent Janie from seeing their faces, it had to have occurred to him that Hargus was lying.

But Jack did believe the man's claim the he'd been involved in the kidnapping in only the most peripheral way. He already knew Bradley Chilcott and Mike Hargus had orchestrated the scheme and he knew why, and this man didn't strike Jack as the type who could be useful to a political campaign in any way, not even in the arena of security/dirty tricks like Hargus.

He'd obviously been added to the team by Hargus at the last minute. Chilcott might not even know.

"Please," the man whispered.

Jack leaned down and rifled through Hargus's pockets, ignoring the other man for the time being. He removed cash and car keys from one pocket—nothing he cared about there—but nestled at the bottom of the other pocket was a pair of micro cassette tapes.

*Interesting.*

Jack stuffed the cash and keys back inside Hargus's pocket. The tapes he slipped into a zippable breast pocket in his survival gear.

Next he lifted Hargus's wallet out of his back pocket and rifled through it. He was unsurprised to find it mostly empty. No credit cards. No driver's license. Nothing that could be used as a form of identification.

Then he noticed a small slip of paper inside the section of the wallet where paper money would have gone had Hargus bothered to use it. He lifted the paper clear and examined it. Jotted on one side in ink was the following: *Chil res,* followed by a series of five random-looking numbers. The other side was blank.

Jack studied the slip of paper. Smiled slightly. *Your boss would be very angry if he knew about this,* Jack thought, and then unzipped the pocket into which he'd placed the microcassette tapes. He added the piece of paper and then zipped the pocket securely closed again.

He returned the wallet to Hargus's trousers and then stepped behind Hargus's accomplice. He placed a hand under each armpit and dragged the man clear of the dead body.

He wasn't gentle.

The man gasped in pain but offered no complaint. Smart move on his part.

Jack leaned the shooting victim against the base of the counter next to the cookstove. Then he searched the man's front pockets, exactly as he had done with Hargus.

It didn't take long and he found nothing of interest.

He crossed his arms and met the man's gaze for a moment, then said, "Lean forward."

"What?"

Jack bent and yanked him by the shoulders. He yelped in pain and as he did, Jack reached behind him and deftly removed a wallet from his rear pocket. What he found confirmed the man's insistence that he was nothing more than a hired thug. He found a driver's license.

There was no way Hargus, or any experienced operator, would have been foolish enough to carry an ID to this cottage. Jack knew he could search the rest of the night and he would find nothing implicating a "Michael Hargus" in any way.

He lifted the license from the wallet and examined it under the light of his phone. Looked from the photograph to the man's face and then back again.

"Byron Hunt, huh? That your real name or a fake? And I strongly suggest you tell the truth."

The man's eyes fell and his shoulders slumped. Given the location of his bullet wound it had to be painful.

He sighed. "It's real."

Jack nodded. "Well, Mr. Byron Hunt of…" he made a show of memorizing the address listed on the license "…Eight Five Seven Melrose Avenue, Albany, New York, I'm going to take this little girl and disappear. You're on your own as far as getting out of here goes, but if I ever see you again, if our paths cross even in the most random manner, I am going to finish you and you'll never see it coming. Am I making myself clear, Mr. Byron Hunt of Albany, New York?"

"I get it," he said. "The last thing I want in this world is to ever see you again, anyway, *or* the little girl for that matter, so you've got nothing to worry about."

"Oh, I know that," Jack shot back. "You're the one who should be worried." His head was pounding and the blood continued to flow slowly down the side of his face, but he locked eyes with Byron Hunt until Hunt dropped his gaze first.

Then he wheeled and held his phone face-out toward the interior of the cottage. He spotted the three guns that had been dropped in the violence of the confrontation and picked them up off the floor one by one.

He recovered his backpack and threaded the sound suppressor off his Sig. Dropped the suppressor into the pack and zipped it closed. Shrugged the pack over his shoulders. Slipped his gun into its shoulder holster and stuffed the other two into the waistband of his trousers.

Then he hurried to Janie. She remained in the fetal position, but she was moaning softly and her eyelids fluttered. She would be regaining consciousness soon and when she did, Jack didn't want her anywhere near the dead man or his accomplice.

He bent and scooped her up in his arms. He felt like he'd been run over by a truck after absorbing several punches flush in the face from Mike Hargus, but she still felt light and insubstantial. In seconds he had crossed the room.

When he arrived at the doorway he turned one last time toward

Byron Hunt. "The minute I get away from here, I'm calling the cops. Unless you want to face a lot of questions you can't answer, I suggest you muster up the strength to grab Hargus's keys and drive his stolen car the hell out of here."

He spun on his heel and plunged through the door without waiting for a response.

He stumbled across the small front yard, turning right when he reached the road and moving as fast as he dared toward the clearing where he'd stashed his truck.

The going was slow, as the pavement was nearly as rutted as the sandy yard he'd just left, and a broken or sprained ankle at this point would likely land him in prison. He still hadn't seen a single vehicle pass along the road, but kept a sharp eye out for approaching headlights anyway.

Janie continued to moan, becoming more active in Jack's arms. Without warning she flailed her arms and legs and they almost went down in a heap.

She opened her eyes. They were wide and confused and terrified. "Where am I? What's going on?"

Jack hugged her to his chest. "You're okay, Tiger. I'm taking you home to your mom where you belong."

"I get to go home? To see Mommy?" Her voice broke and Jack hugged her tighter.

"Yes, Janie, you get to go home to your mommy. And guess what the first thing is I'm going to tell her?"

"What?"

"I'm going to tell her how brave you were. I'm going to tell her your new nickname is 'Tiger' because you're as brave as any tiger that ever roamed the jungle."

"I don't want to go back there, Jack. Those men were mean."

"You don't have to go back there, Janie. Not now, not ever. And I promise you those men will never bother you again."

"I knew you would come for me."

Jack felt himself tearing up. He wouldn't have thought it possible to hug the little girl any tighter than he already was, but somehow he managed it.

He couldn't answer for a moment.

Then he swallowed heavily and said, "I'm sorry it took me so long, Tiger."

# 31

Janie was still awake when they reached Jack's truck, despite the fact it was nearly four-thirty a.m. She complained of a slight headache, but seemed to be thinking and speaking clearly. If she had suffered a concussion from being thrown into the wall when Jack tackled Hargus, it was a mild one.

He unlocked the rear door in the Quad Cab pickup and began settling Janie onto the bench seat when she shook her head firmly. It had to be painful if she'd suffered even a minor concussion.

"I don't want to be back here by myself," she said. "Can't I ride up front with you?"

"Aren't you tired? We have more than a two-hour ride. It will be a lot easier to sleep back here."

Another firm head shake. "I wanna be up front. I don't want to be by myself. Please?"

He smiled and opened his arms again, and she crawled into them gratefully.

When he'd moved her to the front seat he said, "I'll be right back. I just have to clear the brush away from the front of the truck so we can get out of here."

Her eyes widened in panic and she said, "Can't I come? Don't leave me alone!"

"I'll be right in front of the windshield, Janie. You'll be able to see me the entire time, okay?"

She shook her head doubtfully. Her lower lip trembled and she reached for Jack's arm, clamping onto it with vice-grip hands.

Jack snapped his fingers. "Oh my gosh," he said. "I almost forgot."

"Almost forgot what?"

"I brought a friend to keep you company on the way home. He's been very worried about you, so you might have to hug him really tightly."

"A friend? Who?" The fear was gone, replaced by a look of confused curiosity.

He gently pried her fingers from his arm and reached behind the driver's seat, lifting a massive stuffed bear out of a duffel bag. Janie's jaw dropped comically as Jack placed the bear on the seat next to Janie. They were almost exactly the same size.

"Your mom's going to kill me when she sees how big he is," Jack whispered conspiratorially. "But when I saw him in the store and told him about you, he begged to be your new friend and I didn't have the heart to say no."

"He begged?"

"Oh, yeah," Jack said. "There was begging and pleading and even a little crying. It was quite a scene. I was afraid the store people were going to throw us both out."

Janie giggled and hugged her bear.

"You think about what you want to name your new friend while I clean off the truck," Jack said. "Remember, you'll be able to see me the whole time I'm out there, and it will only take a minute. Then we can get going, okay?"

She nodded. "Okay. But I already know what I'm going to name him."

"You've just met him. You picked out a name already?"

Janie nodded.

"What is it?"

"Jack."

His tears were mostly gone by the time he finished clearing the brush away.

* * *

Jack opened the driver's side door to find Janie rocking impatiently in the seat, her arms wrapped around her bear's neck. If the stuffed animal had been alive, she'd be suffocating it.

"When do I get to see Mommy?" she whispered.

"Two hours, Tiger." Jack fired up the Ram and began easing out of the forest and back onto the narrow trail.

"That's a long time," she said.

"I'll bet she'd love to hear from you."

"Yeah," Janie agreed half-heartedly.

"Would you like to call her or are you too tired to talk?"

"We can call her?"

"We sure can." Jack pulled out his phone and punched in his home number. He doubted Edie would mind being awakened before five a.m. under the circumstances—assuming she was even sleeping at all, which seemed unlikely—and guessed this might be the last time she would ever take a call from him.

It was answered on the second ring. "Jack? Is everything alright?"

He handed the phone to Janie, who screamed, "Mommmyyyyy!"

Edie shrieked. The sound was so loud he hoped she hadn't just blown out her child's eardrum. "Janie! Are you okay, baby girl? Are you hurt?"

"I'm okay, Mommy. I just have a headache from when Jack threw me against the wall."

After a moment of shocked silence, Edie answered. She'd lowered the decibel level, though, and Jack could no longer hear her end of the conversation.

After a moment Janie said, "It's okay, Mom. He was busy beating up the bad guys." She sounded so grown-up, Jack glanced across the seat to reassure himself she hadn't somehow fallen out of the truck and been replaced by a teenager.

The little girl and her mother talked a while longer and Janie's head began to sink onto her chest. She dropped off to sleep mid-sentence and the phone plopped onto the seat next to her.

Jack picked it up and said, "She's doing really well, considering what she's been through."

"When will you have her back?"

"Less than two hours."

"Please hurry."

\* \* \*

Jack eased into his driveway in the muted light of an overcast New Hampshire morning. The previous night's clear skies had been replaced by angry-looking storm clouds the color of a fresh bruise.

Before he'd made it halfway to his garage, the front door flew open and Edie Tolliver charged through it like she'd been shot out of a cannon. She sprinted across his yard barefoot, dressed in shorts and a t-shirt and Jack's terrycloth robe, which she'd left untied and which billowed behind her as she ran. He was still moving when she reached the truck and yanked at the door handle and he jerked to a stop, worried about driving over her feet.

The dome light flashed on as the door opened, and Janie opened bleary eyes and blinked rapidly. Then she saw her mother and screamed, and then Edie screamed, and then they were both screaming as they held onto each other like survivors of the Titanic, perfectly content to be half-in and half-out of an idling pickup in the chill of a late-May northern New England morning.

# 32

Bradley Chilcott's eyes were glued to the large-screen high-definition television in the corner of his office. The TV had been placed atop an antique cherry cabinet with the screen angled toward his desk, perfect for watching porn or—as was the case this morning—CNN.

He'd been eating breakfast and drinking coffee when the call came in from one of Governor Studds's staffers telling him to get his ass to the TV and turn on the news.

He'd asked why and the staffer said, "Just do it. Now."

That was no way for a lowly staff puke to speak to an elected official and the number two man in the Maryland hierarchy. Bradley's immediate and instinctive reaction had been to bite the man's head off, to threaten him with suspension or even removal from his job for that kind of impudence, but something in the man's tone stopped him.

Now he knew why the staffer had seemed so upset.

Acting on an anonymous tip early this morning, authorities had found Bradley Chilcott's Chief of Security, Mike Hargus, dead inside his family's vacation cottage on the northern shore of New Hampshire's Lake Winnipesaukee. The New Hampshire State Police were terming the circumstances surrounding his death "suspicious."

Details were sketchy and the official police spokesman—who was popping up every fifteen goddamned minutes on Headline News—wasn't giving out much in the way of concrete information.

Still, Bradley was able to gather the scene was violent and bloody.

And that the condition of Mike Hargus's remains would not translate well to television screens.

For his part, Bradley didn't need specifics to piece together what had happened. That damned fool Hargus had gotten careless and somehow led Jack Sheridan—ex-military Black Ops specialist and current professional assassin—straight to his supposedly secure hideaway. The place nobody in the whole world would be able to find because nobody knew about it.

Apparently Hargus had been wrong on that score. Sheridan had staged an assault on the cottage and recovered his girlfriend's daughter. Bradley knew he'd been successful at getting the kid back because nowhere in the news reports was any mention made of a little girl.

Bradley sipped a mug of herbal tea and considered the implications of this development as he monitored the TV closely, alert for any breaking information.

The first implication was obvious: the planned assassination of Governor Jim Studds was off, for the foreseeable future and probably forever.

Of a more immediate concern was the fact that both the news media and the police would soon—very soon—be asking Bradley a lot of questions, ones to which he'd better have acceptable answers if he didn't want to find himself being tainted politically and personally by Hargus's death.

He was a little surprised the phone hadn't already begun ringing, or that a police investigator hadn't already shown up at his front door.

On the TV another live broadcast was being beamed from Lake Winnipesaukee, this one an aerial shot taken from a helicopter circling over the crime scene. There was nothing new to report, but the media had fixated on the story and Bradley knew he would have to ride out what would likely be an uncomfortable forty-eight to seventy-two hours.

Or more.

Bradley decided he would probably be okay. His staff at the state house had already informed media sources that Chief of Security Mike Hargus had been away from his job on a much-needed vacation, and Bradley intended to be no more specific than that when he took his turn on the hot seat.

After all, Hargus was just another civil servant, one of thousands of men and women employed by the State of Maryland. He'd been a fairly high-level employee; that much was true.

But there was absolutely no reason for anyone to think Bradley Chilcott would ever have discussed the man's private life with him. The lieutenant governor was a busy man, why would the subject of how an employee chose to spend his free time even have come up? He certainly could not be expected to provide any insight into what sort of trouble Hargus may have gotten into while away from his official duties.

That would be Bradley's story, and he would stick to it come hell or high water. He tried to pick it apart and couldn't envision any way the authorities could disprove it.

He was actually more concerned about the media than about law enforcement. The police would treat him with kid gloves thanks to his standing in the community. They might be suspicious that something was not quite right. They probably would, in fact. But suspicions were irrelevant unless they could be backed up with hard evidence a prosecuting attorney could use to gain a conviction in court, and Bradley was one hundred percent certain they would possess no such evidence.

Dealing with the jackals in the media would be a completely separate issue, however. They were under no obligation to consider only prosecutable evidence when reporting a story. They could run with whatever embarrassing or damaging angle they wished. If they chose to, the media could destroy Bradley Chilcott, and in ways even the police couldn't manage.

But Bradley hadn't reached a lofty position in Maryland state government by underestimating the power of narrative control. In fact, if there was one thing in the world he understood intuitively it was media relations. And he thought that, if handled properly, this situation might actually be *beneficial* to him.

Bradley would term this situation a "terrible tragedy," both for the family of Mike Hargus and for the people of Maryland collectively. Bradley would vow to fight as long as it took to get to the bottom of Hargus's tragic death and to see his killer brought to justice. His words would be simultaneously inspiring and sympathetic.

He jotted down a note to have a staffer drive out to the home of Hargus's ex-wife to deliver a personal message of sympathy and to offer any assistance the lieutenant governor's office might be able to provide. And to ensure that at least one media outlet was on hand to film the whole thing.

He nodded to himself and smiled.

This event really could turn out to be a publicity bonanza if managed properly. He tried to recall the last time he'd heard his name featured so prominently on the national news and could not. His Q-Rating had to be skyrocketing, and the old cliché about any pub being good pub had become a cliché in the first place because it was *true*.

Granted, some of the coverage would be negative, especially in the beginning. That was inevitable but it also didn't matter. The ugly rumors already swirling around the circumstances of Hargus's death would fade away soon enough, but with the proper media manipulation, Bradley Chilcott's name would not.

If he played his cards right, Bradley decided he might well parlay this unfortunate tragedy into a national standing that would benefit him every bit as much as Jim Studds's death would have. Maybe more.

But there was one more issue to consider.

And it was probably the most important issue.

Would Bradley live long enough to benefit from the national standing he was soon to develop? Did he now need to look over his shoulder for the rest of his life?

Clearly, Jack Sheridan had taken out Hargus. That was obvious and indisputable. There was one critical question Bradley had to consider: was there any possibility Mike had revealed his connection to Bradley Chilcott before dying?

Bradley didn't think so. He'd retained Mike Hargus for so many years despite his many rough edges precisely because the man was as tough as they came. For all his faults, and Hargus had plenty, he knew how to keep his mouth shut.

And if Hargus hadn't given Bradley up, there should be nothing to worry about. The cell they'd used to call Sheridan and his girlfriend after the kidnapping was an untraceable burner phone, and the email they'd sent was even *more* untraceable. It had been encrypted using technology available only to the CIA and NSA.

In lieu of direct proof that Mike Hargus had been working on specific orders from Bradley Chilcott on the kidnapping/assassination plot, Jack Sheridan would be in the same situation as the police, ironically: he would have suspicions but nothing else.

And if that were the case, Bradley decided he would probably be okay. He was lieutenant governor of Maryland, for Christ's sake. It wasn't like some psycho killer was going to just waltz up to him and blow him away, based on nothing more than a vague suspicion.

There was no reason to take chances, though, and the sudden lack of a security chief—at the exact time he most needed one—could represent a major problem. Bradley made a note on his desk blotter to call the Annapolis Police Department and request a temporary security detail until he could marshal something of a more permanent nature from the Maryland State Police.

There would be nothing suspicious about such a request, under the circumstances. Given the bloody and suspicious nature of Hargus's death, no one would think it odd. It might also provide the added benefit of engendering additional public sympathy should the request "accidentally" be leaked to the press.

Bradley leaned back in his chair. He sipped his tea and then sighed softly. When faced with an unexpected event, he had always felt better after developing an action plan, and today was no exception.

It was ironic that Sheridan had killed Mike Hargus when that was exactly what Bradley had been trying to figure out a way to force him to do. He grinned. *Maybe I should have a staffer research Jack Sheridan's home address and send him a fruit basket as a thank you.*

The grin faded away, and Bradley ran a hand over the stubble along his jawline. He hadn't shaved yet and the skin felt like fine-gauge sandpaper. He would still eventually need to hire another chief of security, but that would have to wait until the furor over Hargus's death died down. He could begin his search now, settle on a name, and then convince the man to take the job at the appropriate time.

It would definitely have to be someone with a little less... initiative...than Mike Hargus had displayed.

Bradley's attention returned to the TV. CNN had gotten around to running another live report from the scene of the killing, but the same non-information was being rehashed. Bradley had turned the sound down so he could think, but superimposed along the bottom of the screen was a graphic trailing the words, *Mike Hargus was employed as Chief of Security for Maryland Lieutenant Governor Bradley Chilcott. Was Hargus in New Hampshire on official business? Questions remain...*

Bradley shook his head and forced his eyes away from the report. He reached into his desk drawer and pulled out a blank sheet of writing paper. The graphic had served as a reminder that he would soon be answering some very pointed questions, and it would be to his benefit to prepare as thoroughly as possible.

He began writing bullet points, listing the items he intended to stress when the police—and the media—came calling later today. This wasn't an ideal situation; that much was obvious. But he'd been in tough spots before. They came with the territory if you expected to earn a living in the political arena.

He was confident he could weather this storm as well.

# 33

Jack sat at his kitchen table sipping coffee. He was fighting an intense drowsiness and wanted nothing more than to fall into bed and sleep. The days when he could stay awake and alert for forty-eight-plus hours on a mission and then bounce back quickly were long gone.

But it didn't matter because the point was moot. There was too much left to do to sleep right now.

So he sipped his coffee and closed his eyes.

Thought about Edie and Janie.

Jack had ushered both of them into his house after their tearful reunion in his driveway. He wondered how long they would have stayed where they were, locked in each other's arms in the cab of his truck, had he not taken Edie by the elbow and guided her up the front walkway with Janie in her arms.

*Maybe they'd still be out there. It's only been three hours, after all.* He smiled weakly and took another sip of coffee, still without opening his eyes.

When they'd gotten inside, Edie marched straight to the kitchen and plopped her little girl down at the table. She'd examined every inch of her, looking for injuries, shaking her head grimly when she encountered the bruise on Janie's head but saying nothing.

Janie had resisted the impromptu medical exam, insisting all she needed was to get back to sleep, but Edie had taken her time. She seemed to need to touch her child and feel her presence and reassure herself that Janie really was here and really was safe and mostly unharmed.

Eventually she'd taken a washcloth and cleaned Janie up—more or less—before carrying her to Jack's spare bedroom, where the little girl had fallen asleep almost immediately.

Jack tried to stay out of the way while Edie tended to Janie. He felt awkward, like he was intruding on an intimate family moment, and remained only too aware of the fact that *he* was the reason this emotional reunion had been necessary.

Edie studiously avoided meeting Jack's eyes. She focused her attention on her child and ignored him. After putting Janie to bed she'd finally spoken to him, saying only that she was exhausted and was going to sleep with her child.

Then she'd disappeared. That was more than two-and-a-half hours ago.

He wondered how long the pair would be behind the closed door of his spare bedroom. Probably most of the day, and if that were the case he would be long gone by the time they emerged.

Maybe that would be for the best.

He lifted the coffee cup toward his lips. Before he could take his next sip, the door to the spare bedroom opened and a seven-year-old guided missile exited the room and blasted down the short hallway. He barely had time to set the cup down before she launched herself into his arms, nearly knocking them both out of the chair and onto the floor.

"Whoa, Nellie!" he said. He hugged the little girl tightly and ruffled her hair.

"My name's not Nellie, silly. It's Janie!"

"Oh, that's right." He slapped his forehead. "I don't know why I can't seem to remember that."

"It's probably because you call me Tiger now," she said seriously.

He pretended to think, stroking his chin and then nodding. "I'll bet that's it," he agreed.

He set her down on the chair and stood to get her a glass of juice and some cereal. "Is your mom awake?"

"Yup. She said to tell you she'll be right out."

"Okay." He took one step in the direction of the refrigerator and then pivoted back toward Janie. "Is *her* name Nellie, by any chance?"

Janie dissolved in giggles and Jack's heart broke for the

thousandth time since her kidnapping. He was going to miss this little girl.

* * *

He was just sitting down across the table from Janie when the door to the spare bedroom opened again and Edie stepped into the hallway. She was dressed in jeans and a sweater, and although Jack knew she hadn't showered—the bathroom door was just a few feet away and no one had gone into or out of it—she looked like the most desirable thing he'd ever seen.

Her hair was mussed from tossing and turning, and worry lines that hadn't been there three days ago surrounded her eyes, but he didn't care about any of that.

He watched her approach and swallowed heavily. He didn't know what was about to happen but doubted it would be pleasant.

She sat in the third chair without speaking and waited for Janie to finish her cereal. Then she sent her to the bathroom to shower off the grime of the last three days.

"And I'm going to check when you've finished," she told her. "So do a good job."

The bathroom door closed and at last Edie raised her eyes to meet Jack's.

"Apparently you're quite the hero," she said softly. "Janie can't decide whether you're Superman or Batman the way you swooped in and beat up the bad guys before saving her and bringing her home."

"Batman has a darker history. Seems more appropriate, I guess."

Edie ignored the comment.

"I think you've gained a fan for life," she said. "Not that Janie didn't adore you before."

"I'm just glad she still *has* a life. Hopefully it will be a good, long, healthy one and the last few days will fade in her memory into the obscurity they deserve."

Edie reached across the table, hesitantly, as if uncertain she wanted to fully commit to the act. She took Jack's hands into her own and lowered her gaze. "I can never repay you for getting my baby back, alive and unharmed. I'm going to be in your debt for the rest of my life."

Jack shook his head.

"You owe me nothing, Edie. In fact, the reality is just the opposite. I can never make up for being the reason Janie was put in harm's way in the first place. I was the reason she was taken and for that I'll never forgive myself."

She released his hands and looked up. Her eyes were wet and red-rimmed, her face filled with anguish.

That was his fault, too.

She cleared her throat and opened her mouth to speak.

Closed it.

Sighed.

Opened it again. "Jack, I know you would never intentionally put me or Janie at risk. I know how you feel about me and I know you're every bit as fond of Janie."

"'Fond' doesn't do justice to what I feel, about either of you."

She nodded. "I know. If I had the slightest doubt about your feelings I wouldn't be sitting here right now after all that's happened."

There didn't seem to be anything to say, so Jack said nothing and waited for Edie to continue.

Eventually she did. "The problem I have is not just with what you do for a living, although I don't understand it and it terrifies me. But even more of an issue than that is the fact that you hid such a major part of yourself from me. I understand it's not the sort of thing you can spread around town, but once we got together and started to become close, didn't you feel you owed it to me to come clean? To give me the opportunity to make up my own mind about whether I wanted to be with you or not?"

"Of course," he said without hesitation. "And if I could go back and change anything about my past, I would start there. I haven't allowed myself to get close to anyone for a very long time, and once it started happening with you I was terrified that I would drive you away, that if you learned who—and what—I really am, you'd run screaming for the hills and I'd never see you again.

"The obvious irony," he added wistfully, "is that by hiding my background from you, I've done exactly what I was afraid was going to happen from the beginning: driven you away."

"I'm still sitting here. I haven't gone anywhere."

"Yet."

"I'm very confused, Jack. But if it weren't for your…unusual talents…Janie would have disappeared forever once she was taken, so I can't completely condemn you. She's everything to me, and she's alive to grumble about taking a shower right now because of you. At the same time, I just don't know how to reconcile your… career…with my values and what I want to teach my girl about how to live her life."

"So where does that leave us?" Jack again met Edie's eyes, marveling as he always did at their luminous green.

She shrugged.

Shook her head.

"I honestly don't know. I can't deny what my heart tells me, and I know you as a kind, gentle and compassionate man, not as some cold-blooded assassin."

"But…"

"But…I just don't know."

# 34

Edie packed her things while Janie was finishing up in the shower. She hadn't brought much to Jack's and it only took a few minutes. Less than half an hour later Edie and Janie were ready to go home.

Edie threw her things into the trunk of her car and then everyone stood awkwardly—and quietly—in the driveway.

The goodbyes were abbreviated. Janie leapt into Jack's arms and gave him a tighter hug than a tiny seven-year-old should be able to manage. She didn't understand the sadness but could obviously feel it. She had tears in her eyes as she scrambled into the passenger seat and pulled the door closed, and then it was just Edie and Jack.

She hugged him loosely. Leaned in and kissed him, but on the cheek rather than the lips.

She stretched on her tiptoes and whispered into his ear, "I'll always love you for saving my baby. Goodbye, Jack."

She turned away before he could respond. Then she slipped behind the wheel, slammed her door and started the engine. She backed down the driveway and into the road, accelerating away without a wave or a look back.

Jack stood in the driveway, hands jammed into his pockets, watching until the little car disappeared. He'd spent a lifetime by himself but had never felt this alone.

When it became clear she wasn't going to return, he trudged up the walkway and into his house.

# 35

Jack wanted to hit the road for Maryland immediately. The desire to introduce himself to Mr. Bradley Chilcott was so strong he thought it might reasonably qualify as a compulsion.

But instead, he returned home and flipped on his television. Taking a little time to absorb as much as he could from the news reports about the Mike Hargus killing—especially as it related to Hargus's boss, Bradley Chilcott—could potentially pay big dividends, and Jack was determined not just to see this disaster through to the end, but to do it the right way.

The authorities hadn't wasted any time connecting Hargus to Chilcott, and as Jack sat alone in his living room, the face of Maryland's lieutenant governor filled his TV screen. The man was doing his best to look sincere as he gazed into the cameras and pleaded with viewers for any information that would bring the murderer of his chief of security to justice.

The statement was ludicrous, of course, and Jack laughed out loud despite his rapidly building fury. The last thing in the world Chilcott wanted was for the killing to be solved, because if that happened, *he* would find himself behind bars for the rest of his life.

The reason for Chilcott's press conference was obvious, and it had nothing to do with solving any murder. The lieutenant governor was doing what politicians always did, given the opportunity: grandstanding.

And Jack had to admit the man was smooth. He segued from the search for Hargus's killer right into a solemn promise to bring every last resource of the lieutenant governor's office to bear in order to provide for the widow and her two young sons.

Jack forced himself to ignore Chilcott's words. He looked beyond the man speaking at the podium to focus his attention on the innocent young boys being shamelessly exhibited next to their teary-eyed mother. They didn't look much older than Janie Tolliver.

Jack didn't regret killing Mike Hargus. He'd vowed to do whatever it took to recover Janie unharmed and had done exactly that. No more and no less.

But the fact that the father of two children roughly Janie's age could have been a party to the kidnapping and planned murder of a young girl only served to strengthen his already sincere belief that he'd done the right thing by eliminating the man.

The world was a better place with him gone.

Addition by subtraction.

And Bradley Chilcott had children approximately the same age as well.

Jack thumbed the remote to shut off his television. He sat for a long time staring at a blank screen. Then he stood and began gathering the supplies he would need for a road trip down to Maryland.

It took less than fifteen minutes and Jack was ready to roll. He was always prepared to move at a moment's notice and had long ago learned the value of traveling light.

His skull throbbed from the gash he'd received when his head struck Mike Hargus's cookstove, as well as from the pummeling he'd taken. He knew he needed sutures but wasn't about to waste time going to the hospital. The bruising on his face from Hargus's fists was steadily darkening. His muscles ached and creaked in a constant reminder—not that he needed one—that he was an aging man employed in a young person's occupation.

And even worse than the physical hurt was the mental anguish, the knowledge that he alone had been responsible for the near-ruination not just of one life but two. Because had Janie Tolliver been killed, Edie's life would have been over just as surely as if she too had died at the hands of Mike Hargus.

Jack tossed his duffel bag in front of the door and picked up his phone. He punched in a series of numbers from memory and made the call he'd been considering for a very long time.

\* \* \*

The driving route to Maryland would take Jack directly past Boston, exactly as it had when he traveled to Newark a few days ago. Normally he would bypass the city entirely, circling west of it on Interstate 495, adding a little mileage to the trip but saving time by avoiding the urban congestion.

Not today.

Today he drove straight into the city. Although he *wanted* to get to Maryland as soon as possible, he *needed* to spend a few minutes in the city.

He had business to discuss with Mr. Stanton.

Today's meeting would take place in Boston Common. During all the time he'd been a contractor for The Organization—a period of several years—he'd had but one contact: Mr. Stanton. Jack didn't think they'd ever met in the same place twice, and today was no exception.

He drove to the agreed-upon location near the northwest corner of the park, shut down his truck and started walking. Mr. Stanton would be somewhere nearby but would not reveal himself until he was ready.

The day was cool and overcast but humid, with the threat of thunderstorms looming.

The air felt heavy. Portentous.

Jack ambled along a pathway, moving slowly, hands in his pockets. With rain coming there was little in the way of pedestrian traffic. Jack assumed that was why Mr. Stanton had chosen this spot for their rendezvous.

He rounded a corner and just as he passed the intersection of another pathway, Mr. Stanton was there. He appeared seemingly out of nowhere, falling in next to Jack and matching his pace stride for stride. Bob Fosse couldn't have choreographed the move any better.

"I'm glad things worked out with little Janie," Mr. Stanton said without preamble. He spoke softly but enunciated the words with razor-sharp clarity.

Jack had been dealing with Mr. Stanton for a long time. He knew The Organization was small in number but powerful, with tentacles stretching into virtually all areas of American life; avenues of communication and influence that stretched far beyond what most could imagine.

But this comment caught him off-guard, and he instinctively swiveled his head to stare intently at his walking companion.

Jack's contact smiled, his thin lips forming a nearly bloodless line.

"It is to The Organization's benefit to remain informed," Mr. Stanton said calmly, as they resumed strolling the paths of Boston Common. "And I must say, the world is a far better place now than it was when Michael Hargus was taking up space in it."

He paused, obviously awaiting a response, but Jack had nothing to say.

After a moment he resumed speaking. Jack thought he detected the slightest twinge of disappointment in Mr. Stanton's voice that he hadn't elicited a reaction.

"I'll even hazard a guess as to where you're going next," the man said. "Unless I'm way off base, you're driving down the coast to Annapolis."

Another pause.

More silence from Jack.

"I will admit to being a little confused as to the nature of our meeting, however. My initial thought was that you required some specific equipment or weaponry to complete your little freelance job, something only I could provide with sufficient discretion. But if that were the case, you would have given me those specifics when you set up the meeting."

Jack waited patiently and continued meandering along the pathway.

"So please tell me, Jack, assuming you're eventually going to say *something*: what can The Organization do for you?"

"Nothing."

"Excuse me?"

"You heard me," he said. "I'm finished. Done. Retiring. Giving my notice. Your assumption about where I'm going today and why is right on target, but this will be my final job. I just can't do this anymore."

It was Mr. Stanton's turn to stop in surprise. He stared at Jack, eyebrows raised, and Jack felt a moment's satisfaction that he'd finally shocked the man who was always so well informed he seemed to possess almost supernatural cognitive abilities.

"I understand you've been shaken by the events of the last few days," Mr. Stanton said as they resumed their stroll.

A lone female jogger approached along the path, moving in the opposite direction and steadfastly refusing to meet their eyes. They waited in silence for her to continue out of earshot despite the fact her ears were plugged with iPod buds.

When she had disappeared, Jack said, "You're right, the last few days *have* clarified some things for me. But my decision to retire is about more than just me being responsible for Janie nearly losing her life."

"How so?"

"I'm getting old quickly. My body doesn't recover like it used to. Mike Hargus was bigger, stronger and better conditioned than I was, despite the fact he'd gone mostly to seed. And the results of our encounter are plain to see." He turned and faced Mr. Stanton head-on, to demonstrate to greatest effect the full extent of the beating he'd taken inside the cottage on Lake Winnipesaukee.

"And yet he's occupying a slab at the morgue and you're standing here talking to me."

"Only because I was extremely lucky. And luck eventually runs out."

Mr. Stanton shrugged. "What one would consider luck, another would term the inevitable result of superior experience and preparation."

Jack chuckled. "Let me guess. Debate team champion in college?"

Mr. Stanton returned the smile in silence. It looked contemplative.

"In any event," Jack said, "this isn't open to discussion. My mind can't be changed. I'm here because I wanted to notify you of my decision face-to-face. I felt I owed that to The Organization in general and to you specifically."

"I appreciate that, Jack."

They continued along the pathway. Jack had never visited Boston Common despite being a New England native, but he guessed they were moving in a wide circle and before much longer would arrive back where he'd parked his truck.

The silence was companionable.

After a while Mr. Stanton said, "I trust you'll understand, Mr. Sheridan, if The Organization retains your contact information in our secure computer servers and don't remove your email address from our operatives' roster just yet. Things have a way of changing, oftentimes very quickly, as I think you know better than most."

"This thing won't," Jack said firmly. "I've given it a lot of thought, over a longer period of time than you probably realize, and I'm comfortable with my decision. It's not going to change."

Mr. Stanton smiled again, the skin around his eyes wrinkling in merriment as if he might be enjoying his own private joke. Following his initial shock, he seemed completely unruffled by Jack's announcement.

"I believe this is where you parked upon your arrival," Mr. Stanton said.

Jack looked around and realized his assumption about their walking path had been correct. He could see his truck through a thin screen of trees and arbor.

He turned back toward Mr. Stanton to shake his now-former employer's hand but the man was already walking away. His trench coat flapped lightly in the humid air.

Jack watched as he strolled. He looked like just another elderly man enjoying some air. Eventually he turned a corner and disappeared.

# 36

The city of Annapolis, Maryland, is located south of Baltimore and east of Washington, D.C., hard by the Chesapeake Bay. It has a rich history and was once, long ago and for a brief period, the capitol of colonial America. Chartered by England's Queen Anne in 1708, Annapolis is home to the United States Naval Academy and is Maryland's state capitol.

Jack's travels had never taken him to Annapolis, and as a United States history buff he'd long wanted to see the city.

He would have preferred his first visit to be under different circumstances.

The drive took a little over eight hours after leaving Boston Common. He took his time, staying within shouting distance of the posted speed limit, not so much because he couldn't afford to get stopped by law enforcement as because he couldn't come up with a single reason to hurry.

Bradley Chilcott wasn't going anywhere, and the prospect of returning to New Hampshire to sit alone inside the four walls of his house struck him as singularly unappealing. Edie and Janie Tolliver would only be a couple of miles away but they might as well be a couple thousand.

As expected, traffic was congested along the Cross-Bronx Expressway approaching the George Washington Bridge, but it broke free again as he entered northern New Jersey. The rest of the drive went smoothly.

By nightfall Jack found himself resting in a comfortable

roadside motel—he paid cash and registered under one of his many false identifications—just south of Baltimore. He grabbed a bite to eat and had one drink at an anonymous bar. He was in bed by eleven p.m.

It was important to be rested. Tomorrow he would begin the final job of his career.

# 37

Morning dawned with apparent reluctance. Jack had now spent three days in Annapolis and not once had he seen the sun, the overcast layer impenetrable and a perfect reflection of his mood.

Today he sat around the corner and a few hundred feet away from Lieutenant Governor Bradley Chilcott's home. The three days of surveillance had left him as prepared as he felt he could reasonably be.

The lieutenant governor's mansion was located in one of Annapolis's oldest neighborhoods. Each leafy block contained no more than one or two large, well-maintained homes, the yards immaculate and the streets wide and clean and lined with ancient maple trees.

Jack's most pressing concern had been to identify security. Chilcott's home was being protected twenty-four/seven, a virtually unprecedented condition for a state lieutenant governor. Given the circumstances of Mike Hargus's death it seemed clear a paranoid Chilcott had requested the police presence.

The resulting security seemed largely for show, though. During his surveillance, Jack had spent time in virtually every part of the neighborhood from which he could observe Chilcott's home and he was by now certain that "security" was limited to one officer placed in a cruiser directly across the street from Chilcott's front door.

The officers rotated shifts every eight hours.

And that was it. He hadn't seen any evidence of a second officer entering or leaving the house, and he'd spent sixteen-plus hours a day watching.

The lieutenant governor's wife and two children had left the home at precisely 7:55 a.m. each day so far this week, returning both of the previous days about four o'clock in the afternoon.

The timing of their departure would indicate the woman was dropping the kids off at school. Where she went afterward, and how she spent her day until four o'clock, Jack didn't know, but his Internet research on Bradley Chilcott had revealed two items of importance where the wife was concerned: she was heavily involved in children's charitable causes, and rumors of serial infidelity on her husband's part—among other, darker sexual practices—had swirled for years.

Jack didn't consider himself any more perceptive than the average person, but it didn't take a genius to put two-and-two together in this case. Kim Chilcott spent as much time as she could away from her home and husband because their marriage was a sham.

She was either sticking with him out of a misplaced sense of duty, or he held some kind of leverage over her and was forcing her to stay. After all, it wouldn't do for a politician looking to raise his national profile to undergo a potentially nasty divorce.

None of that mattered to Jack.

All he cared about was that neither the wife nor the children return home unexpectedly today. Barring some unusual occurrence—one of the kids coming home from school sick would be the most likely possibility—he felt reasonably confident that once they exited the house today, his target's family would not be back until late afternoon.

Chilcott himself had maintained a seemingly predictable schedule as well. Both days he'd left his home shortly after the rest of his family and then returned around one p.m. Presumably the man drove to the state house each morning, but apparently there was either very little in the way of real work to occupy a lieutenant governor's time, or he simply wasn't all that motivated.

Again, Jack didn't care which scenario was accurate.

He weighed the advantages of another day or two of surveillance—additional information could not possibly be a bad thing when operating solo—against the potential risks and decided he couldn't afford to hang around this neighborhood any longer.

He'd parked his truck in the lot of a busy shopping mall ten miles away and rented a different car each day. Doing so had allowed him to maintain anonymity, but the fact was that a neighborhood like this represented about the worst-case scenario for conducting surveillance. People tended to pay attention and watch out for their neighbors, and there simply wasn't enough through traffic in the area to allow him to blend in effectively.

Jack had pushed his luck as far as he dared. It was time to proceed.

He watched the house from a safe distance until Kim Chilcott's white Volvo backed out of the driveway and accelerated toward Annapolis. She waggled her fingers to the officer parked across the street and received a half-hearted wave in return.

The tops of two small heads were just visible in the rear window as she passed the cross street on which Jack had parked.

Good. Both children were on their way to school.

Chilcott should now depart within the next few minutes and return shortly after lunchtime.

The house would be empty for several hours.

Chilcott's garage door opened a few minutes later, exactly as anticipated, and the lieutenant governor drove away.

Jack waited a little longer. He expected to see nothing more of interest and didn't.

Eventually he started the rental car and drove off in the direction Kim Chilcott had gone a few minutes earlier.

# 38

Breakfast consisted of hot black coffee. The franchise coffee shop was just off the highway along the route to an office-supply store located roughly halfway between Annapolis and Baltimore. Jack was able to grab the caffeine without wasting more than five minutes in the process.

Leaving Annapolis just to purchase his supplies was undoubtedly overkill—pun definitely intended—since none of the materials Jack needed would be in any way suspicious or memorable, but he couldn't think of a single good reason to take unnecessary chances.

And again, he was in no hurry to rush back to New Hampshire and be alone.

At the office supply store he paid cash for a medium-sized cardboard box and a roll of bright blue packing tape.

He returned to the rental car and folded the box together while sitting in the parking lot. Then he picked up a couple of decent-sized rocks and dropped them inside the box for stability's sake. He closed the cover and taped it securely shut, then reinforced the corners and edges of the box with the tape. He did so not to protect the box but to make it as visible and eye-catching as possible.

When finished, he leaned back and inspected his little arts-and-crafts project with a critical eye.

Shrugged.

He supposed it would do; it only had to fool a few people for a few minutes to accomplish his goal. After that it would become irrelevant.

He left the lot and drove to a corner convenience store a block away. Bought a prepaid cell phone, the cheapest he could find. It would only be used twice before being discarded forever.

Back in his car, he examined his supplies and reviewed his game plan, searching for flaws. The plan itself was nothing complicated, but given the constraints he was operating under and the lack of proper preparation, he guessed it was about as solid as he could hope for.

*I suppose I'll find out.*

\* \* \*

The long-threatened storm had finally arrived while Jack was buying his supplies, and now a cold, hard mid-Atlantic rain pelted his windshield.

He hoped the sudden downpour wasn't an omen.

Decided not to think about it.

He returned to Bradley Chilcott's neighborhood via a route that would funnel him to a point well north of the police cruiser he knew would still be stationed outside the lieutenant governor's home. It had been important to remain anonymous before. It was critical now.

He knew he would find what he was looking for relatively close to Chilcott's home and he was right. Two blocks away and around the corner, to be precise, a maroon SUV sat at the curb. It was parked halfway between two driveways and directly beneath one of the massive old maple trees dotting the neighborhood.

The car was empty.

The neighborhood was quiet.

Jack picked up the cardboard box he'd constructed earlier and stepped out of the rental car. The rain slanted at an angle, splashing off the pavement as he moved to the SUV. He ignored the deluge and bent almost to the ground, tossing the package under the big vehicle, aiming for a spot beneath the center of the car. It skidded to a stop more or less where he had hoped and he nodded, satisfied with the result.

He turned and walked back to his rental. Climbed behind the wheel and started the engine. Drove slowly back in the direction from which he'd come just minutes earlier. He circled the neighborhood, giving Chilcott's house a wide berth, and then eased to a stop a block west of his target's empty home. He was now almost directly opposite the maroon SUV with the package on the wet road beneath it.

Jack eased the car forward until he could just make out the police cruiser through his side window. It was a block-and-a-half away. A row of neatly trimmed shrubs ran along the property line, shielding Jack's car from view of the officer inside the cruiser.

*Perfect.*

He lifted his burner phone off the front seat and punched in a number he'd memorized earlier. The call was answered on the second ring.

"Annapolis Police." The voice was clipped and professional.

"Yes, hello," Jack said, putting just the slightest hesitation into his voice. "Uh, I live at Seventy-Two Elm here in Annapolis and I'm calling to report a suspicious package under my car."

"Suspicious package?"

"That's right. I stopped at home for a few minutes and when I went back outside I spotted a good-sized box under my car. It definitely wasn't in the road when I arrived and it looks like it was placed there intentionally. I'm a divorce attorney and my line of work unfortunately earns me plenty of enemies. I think something's wrong. Could you send an officer to check it out, please? I'd be very grateful."

The dispatcher sounded uninterested and unconvinced of the severity of the situation, but she promised to send an officer. He thanked her and disconnected the call.

Now he just had to wait. It shouldn't take long.

Police departments everywhere were terminally short-handed. Jack was banking on the fact that the officer standing duty outside Chilcott's home would be bored and tired of staring at Bradley Chilcott's closed front door. He would hear the address being broadcast by the dispatcher and realize he was only a block or so away.

He would volunteer to go check out the suspicious package. The neighborhood was deserted, Chilcott was off at work and why the hell did the lieutenant governor need twenty-four/seven protection on an empty house anyway? The officer would reason that he would be away from his position outside the Chilcott home for maybe three minutes, and then he'd return to his location after clearing the call.

Hell, he would damned near be within sight of Chilcott's home the entire time.

He would get to do something at least moderately more interesting than his current assignment, and none of the patrol officers actually on duty would have to waste their time checking out what was almost certainly a false alarm.

Everybody wins.

It was simple human nature, and Jack was confident his plan would work. If not, if his assumptions about the police officer sitting in his car a hundred or so feet away were proven wrong, he would implement a second plan: stage a car accident down the street to draw the officer's attention, something he *couldn't* ignore. Then Jack would slip quietly away in the resulting confusion.

He hoped that wouldn't be necessary. It was too public for his taste and he also hated involving innocent people—or their property—any more than was absolutely necessary.

But he would do it if he had to.

\*    \*    \*

He didn't.

Less than two minutes after Jack disconnected the call to the Annapolis Police, the light bar began flashing atop the cruiser parked across the street from the Chilcott home. The car eased away from the curb, executed a slow U-Turn in the wide, empty road, and then rolled down the block. It turned the corner and moved out of sight in the direction of Jack's box of rocks sitting under the SUV on Elm Street.

Jack waited with his left hand resting on the door handle. The moment the cruiser disappeared he was up and moving. He picked his briefcase off the passenger seat and stepped into the driving rain.

He was dressed in a conservative charcoal-grey suit, with a blue tie over a crisp white Oxford shirt. A long black topcoat and fedora shielded him—more or less—from the elements, not to mention from any security cameras that might stand between his rental car and Bradley Chilcott's home. He double-timed down the sidewalk, more because he knew the officer he'd lured away from his station would be back soon than because he was bothered by the weather.

The reality was that he was grateful for the heavy rain. No one who happened to glance out their living room window would think it odd to see a grown man hurrying past in these conditions.

Water splashed his shoes and soaked his socks as avoiding puddles on the sidewalk proved impossible. He reached Chilcott's walkway and hurried up to the front door.

He slipped on a pair of nitrile gloves, then removed his lock-pick gun from the pocket of his overcoat and got to work. Thirty seconds later he had picked both door locks and stood inside the open foyer, dripping water onto a beautifully polished hardwood floor.

He looked to the right of the entrance and saw nothing. Looked immediately left and found what he had known must be here. Built into the wall was a small electronic control panel with a keypad featuring digits numbered one to ten. A speaker in the panel had begun emitting a series of loud beeps, three at a time followed by a one-second break, then three more beeps followed by another short break. A small red LED had begun flashing next to the keypad.

Jack reached into his pocket and removed the slip of paper he'd taken from Mike Hargus's wallet back at the Lake Winnipesaukee cottage. On it was written *Chil res,* followed by a series of five random-looking numbers.

Jack had deduced immediately what the slip of paper represented. As Bradley Chilcott's Chief of Security, Hargus had had access to the Chilcott home in the event of an emergency requiring his assistance. The numbers represented the code to disarm the alarm system, but the security officer had been too lazy to memorize it.

He'd slipped it into his wallet and forgotten about it.

And now the laziness of a dead man was going to permit Jack to complete his mission. He punched the series of numbers in sequential order into the keypad. Instantly the audible alarm ceased. The red light stopped flashing and instead a green LED next to it began to glow steadily.

Jack was in. He dropped the alarm code back into his pocket and stood still, facing the interior of the home, taking in his surroundings. The place felt empty. Abandoned.

He breathed deeply and moved through the house, familiarizing himself with the layout and confirming he was, in fact, alone inside. Then he rummaged around the kitchen until finding a drawer filled with dishtowels. He grabbed on and sopped up the mess he'd made on the foyer floor, then tossed the towel back into the drawer.

Housework complete, Jack moved to the living room and glanced out the big picture window to see that the space previously occupied by the police sentry remained empty. This was a bit surprising. He'd expected the officer to have cleared the call regarding the suspicious package by now and returned to his previous location.

The sound of sirens floated through the walls, relatively far away but closing fast. The responding officer must have been concerned enough about Jack's cardboard box to call in the bomb squad.

Odd, considering the complainant would have been nowhere to be found. Irrelevant to Jack's purposes as well. But once those specialized responders arrived on the scene and were briefed, the officer would presumably return to his spot across the street.

Not that it mattered now. Jack's diversion had worked like a charm.

# 39

Jack checked his watch.

It was straight-up noon.

He guessed he had an hour, give or take, before Bradley Chilcott's abbreviated workday came to an end.

Hopefully the lieutenant governor would come straight home after lunch as he had done each of the previous two days and not pick today to cut the ribbon at the opening of a new shopping mall, or give a talk at a junior high school, or rent a motel room and screw an intern.

There would be no way to know for sure until the man's car turned into his driveway. In the meantime, Jack had plenty of prep work with which to occupy himself.

He moved straight to Chilcott's study. Presumably this was where the target spent the majority of his time, which meant this was where Jack would concentrate the majority of his preparations.

It was a beautiful workspace; he could understand why Chilcott would want to come home early every day. A massive working fireplace took up most of one wall, while floor-to-ceiling bookshelves covered the others. The shelves were filled with mostly non-fiction volumes on virtually every conceivable subject of interest to a political pro.

The portion of the hardwood floor that Jack could see gleamed with a luster every bit as brilliant as the floor in the foyer, but a plush Persian rug covered most of the room. Its deep wine-colored pattern, set against a rich cream background, contrasted nicely with the room's dark wood tones to create a sense of warmth.

Jack wondered absently how much the carpet was worth. Probably more than he made in a year, he decided.

A maple desk occupied one corner of the room, angled to allow Chilcott an unobstructed view of the doorway. On top of the desk sat a telephone, a computer and a Tiffany lamp. A large-screen HDTV had been placed in the opposite corner of the office.

Next to the door was a small, overstuffed couch. A pair of throw pillows bearing the official seal of the State of Maryland had been placed on it, one inside each armrest.

It was impressive. Professional but comfortable. Jack assumed this was where Chilcott and Hargus had hatched their plot to use an innocent young girl as leverage to force a political assassination, and he began to become consumed by the smoldering rage he'd felt intermittently since answering Edie's panicked phone call five days ago.

He dragged his thoughts away from the kidnapping and forced himself to concentrate on the situation at hand. It was critical he remain clear-headed if he expected to finish this thing and get out alive.

He seated himself at Chilcott's desk and rifled through the drawers. There were two on the left side, as well as a single narrow drawer located below the desk's writing surface. The side drawers were wide and deep and contained personal financial statements and similar legal documents.

It became quickly apparent there was nothing of interest inside them. It wasn't surprising. The man would have to be a colossal fool to store potentially incriminating evidence in his home office. And whatever else Jack thought of Bradley Chilcott, he didn't consider the man a fool.

He turned his attention to the middle drawer. It was locked, which instantly made it the most interesting. Jack thought he had a pretty good idea what he would find when he picked the lock.

Seconds later he discovered his guess was right on target.

He chuckled and stood. Walked to the couch, upon which he'd placed his briefcase. Opened the case and removed one item.

He returned to the desk and in seconds had made a small adjustment to one of the drawer's contents. Then he slid the drawer closed and relocked it, and continued his search of Bradley Chilcott's office.

By the time he'd finished he rechecked his watch. If Chilcott kept to his schedule of the last couple of days, he should be returning home any time now.

Jack left the office and descended the stairs to the first floor. Moved to the front window and glanced outside. The Annapolis Police cruiser was back across the street, the officer inside maintaining a vigilant, three hundred sixty degree scan of the area.

The sentry was being very conscientious.

Jack decided he'd never felt so safe.

# 40

Bradley Chilcott stepped into the foyer and felt a flash of anger at the silence that accompanied his arrival. His fury was immediate and visceral, and unfortunately not unexpected.

Kim had fucked up.

Again.

*Goddammit!*

A series of jarring beeps should have filled the first floor the moment he opened the door. Once that happened, Bradley would have thirty seconds to enter the proper code into the alarm panel before a siren would begin wailing, with automatic notification to the Annapolis Police that a break-in was in progress at the Chilcott home.

It was a quality alarm system. Bradley had paid a lot of money for the installation a few years ago at Mike Hargus's suggestion. But the fucking thing was useless if you forgot to set it, and his worthless bitch of a wife had overlooked the damned thing again.

*Jesus Christ. And now of all times, with Jack Sheridan running around, doing who knows what, after killing Hargus and rescuing his girlfriend's kid.*

Granted, Kim knew nothing about the Tolliver kidnapping/ Studds assassination scheme, but still, Bradley had stressed time after time how important it was to set the alarm whenever she left the house, and at least a third of the time she forgot to do it.

She was as scatterbrained as they came. Bitch.

Thank God for the Annapolis Police officer stationed outside the house. Even without a functional alarm system he knew he had nothing to worry about.

This time.

But Kim would still pay for her error; Bradley would make good and goddamned sure of that. Every once in a while the stupid cow needed to be reminded of her place, and that time had clearly arrived again.

But wait a second.

Hadn't Kim left the house *before* Bradley today? Or was that yesterday? The day before?

He thought he remembered her shouting up the stairs as he was getting dressed that she was leaving to bring the kids to school and then heading off to whatever charitable foundation she was wasting time at this week.

He scratched his chin. Shook his head. That must have been yesterday, because *he* sure as hell would not have walked into the garage without setting the alarm.

The aspiring presidential candidate walked into the kitchen, still deep in thought, and hung his topcoat over a chair to drip-dry. The rain had been torrential as he left work and walked to his car. The coat would leave a mess all over the floor but Kim could clean it up later.

He made a mental note to remind her to do it *before* the beating. Afterward she wouldn't be moving too well.

He'd eaten a sandwich before leaving the state house so he wasn't hungry. He *was* thirsty, however. Even though it was barely past noon, Bradley strode to the fully stocked bar in the corner of the living room and dropped three ice cubes into a glass. Added three fingers of Chivas. He was tempted to keep going, to fill the goddamned glass to the brim, but it *was* only one p.m., so he would be a good boy and limit his intake.

For now.

He'd always been a heavy drinker, but lately even he knew he'd begun to go off the rails where alcohol was concerned. But knowing something and being able to control his compulsion to keep doing that something were two completely separate and—in his case at least—mostly unrelated issues.

He promised himself he would get his drinking under control

once things got back to normal. But between the stress of planning the Studds assassination and now the added stress of the plan turning to shit, Bradley really needed the positive reinforcement provided by a fuzzy alcohol buzz.

It was false reinforcement; he knew that, just as he knew he'd been making the same lame promise to slow his drinking for far too long. But now was not the time to deal with either consideration.

Bradley lifted the glass to his lips and felt the first sip of liquid heaven burn its way down his throat as the ice cubes tinkled musically in the glass. When he was on the campaign trail and people asked whether he believed in God, his stock answer was, "How else do you explain good scotch?"

The quip never failed to earn a laugh, but Bradley wondered what people would think if they knew he was mostly serious.

He treated himself to a second sip and then began wandering upstairs to his study. He wasn't looking forward to the rest of the day, because most of it would be spent sorting through the short list of candidates he'd identified as potential replacements for Mike Hargus as security chief.

The work would be dry and boring. But it would also ensure the smooth progression of his career. He had to be careful not to saddle himself with a guy who possessed the wrong temperament. He didn't want to end up facing the same problem he'd just escaped with Hargus: a man too ambitious for his own good.

He wandered into his study, contemplating the irony of being saved from his Hargus problem by Jack Sheridan, and crossed the room to his desk.

Bradley Chilcott wasn't a gun man. Didn't like them. Didn't believe in them, even though he had to feign support for the Second Amendment during the election cycle if he wanted to avoid becoming an *ex*-politician.

He only owned a gun to protect himself, because everyone knew how unpopular political figures could be, and every once in a while some unhinged moron tried to act on his hatred. But he *did* own one. He hadn't practiced much with it, but he'd used it enough to understand the basics of a semi-automatic handgun's operation.

Enough to recognize the *ch-chunk* of exactly that type of gun's slide being racked behind him.

He froze.

Somewhere in the back of his instantly terrified mind, Bradley was proud of himself. He didn't spill a single drop of his Chivas.

# 41

"A little early for happy hour, don't you think?"

Jack held his gun loosely, aimed in the general direction of Bradley Chilcott. He didn't need the weapon to keep Chilcott in line but wanted to ensure the man's attention didn't wander. Jack had faced the business end of a pistol enough times to know the menacing sight would accomplish that goal quite nicely.

The lieutenant governor looked like a statue. He stood stiffly at his desk facing away from Jack, who was seated on the overstuffed couch next to the door. One State of Maryland pillow flanked him on each side.

"Who are you and what do you want?"

"Come on, Brad, you must have a pretty good idea. You're supposed to be a smart guy, who do you think I am?"

"I prefer to be addressed as Bradley," he said curtly, as if the pronunciation of his name was his biggest problem. "And I have no clue who you are. What I *do* know is this: you're in big trouble. The police are literally right outside my door."

"I'm well aware of that, *Brad*, and I'm very grateful for their presence. That officer parked outside should ensure that you and I have the privacy and the uninterrupted time together we need."

"We need no time together. Why don't you just tell me what you want so you can be on your way?"

"That's not very hospitable, considering I came all the way from New Hampshire to see you." Jack smiled as Chilcott's shoulders slumped.

"That's right," he continued. "New Hampshire. I thought since you and your recently deceased chief of security went to all the trouble of kidnapping an innocent child and threatening her murder just to get my attention, the least I could do is give you some of it."

"I don't know what you're talking about, but you'd better—"

"Knock it off, Brad. Right now. I mean it."

Chilcott's voice cracked and his jaw snapped shut. The back of his neck flushed brightly, either out of anger or fear. Jack couldn't tell which and didn't care.

Silence fell over the room and Jack allowed it to linger before continuing to speak.

When he did, his voice was almost a whisper. "We're far beyond lame denials and claims of innocence. A 'not guilty' plea might work in a criminal trial, but you may have noticed there's no jury here today. I know exactly what you did, and I'm here *because of* what you did."

Chilcott huffed but said nothing.

"I feel like we got off on the wrong foot," Jack said, "so let's start over. Please allow me to introduce myself. I'm Jack Sheridan."

The man's entire body tensed at the words, although by now they couldn't have come as any surprise. Even an idiot would have known who was pointing a gun at him from the moment he heard the slide rack.

And Bradley Chilcott was no idiot.

Jack placed his gun on the couch next to him and folded his hands in his lap. "Look at me, Brad."

Chilcott turned slowly, rotating on the balls of his feet like the world's oldest and most out of shape ballet dancer. It was clear he expected to have his head blown off at any moment. When he saw that Jack wasn't even holding his gun, he wrinkled his forehead in confusion.

"You look awfully uncomfortable standing all stiff and tense over there, Brad," Jack continued. "Let's not be so formal, since we're getting to know each other and all. Feel free to take a load off. Have a seat at your desk if you'd like."

Chilcott's eyes narrowed in suspicion. It was obvious he thought Jack was trying to trick him somehow. But he moved, ever so slowly, behind his desk and sat. The chair creaked and groaned.

They stared at each other for a moment and then, more comfortable behind his desk and emboldened by the changing circumstances, Chilcott tried to take control.

"First of all," he said, "I have no idea what you're referring to with the paranoid fantasy you seem to be having about my involvement in the kidnapping of some little girl."

"Is that so?"

"Yes, that's so, but I'm not finished. The second thing I wanted to say is that I consider myself a reasonable man. If you stand up and get the hell out of my house right this minute I'll consider not pressing charges. I might be willing to overlook this entire incident."

Jack pretended to consider the offer. He put a serious look on his face and paused for a moment.

"That's quite a generous offer," he said, "considering I broke into your home and held you at gunpoint. That's a pretty serious 'incident.'"

Chilcott held Jack's gaze steadily.

"You're willing to just let bygones be bygones, is that it?"

"As I said, I consider myself a reasonable man." The words came out hesitantly, Chilcott's air of authority already beginning to fracture.

"Well, as much as I appreciate your very kind offer, I think I'll have to decline. I worked hard to get in here and I'm exactly where I want to be. I'm not leaving until our business is finished."

"Wh-what business is that?" Chilcott had never put his whiskey glass down and now he lifted it to his lips and took a sip that was more of a gulp. His hand was shaking badly.

"I'm here to help you."

"Help me? How could you help me? Other than by leaving, that is."

Jack smiled. He opened his briefcase and pretended to search for something. Then he muttered, "Ah, here we are."

He withdrew a small, battery-powered microcassette player and tiny tape. Closed the briefcase. Used it as a small table upon which he placed the tape player.

He looked at Chilcott and smiled. "These things aren't too

common anymore. I had to go to a couple of office supply places before I found one. Everybody uses computer flash drives and similar devices now, but I guess your sadly departed friend Mike Hargus was more old school than that. But it's okay, we all have to adapt and overcome sometimes, isn't that right, Brad?"

Chilcott had gone silent again. He stared at the tape player like he'd never seen one before. His concern about what might be on the tape was palpable.

"Anyway," Jack continued, "I suspected you might begin to experience sudden memory loss during our impromptu meeting, so I came prepared to address your amnesia."

Chilcott's eyes darted between the tape player and Jack's face.

Back and forth.

Back and forth.

"Imagine my surprise," Jack said, "when I searched your chief of security's body following our...disagreement...and found this little insurance policy."

He looked sadly into the lieutenant governor's eyes and said, "I hate to have to break this to you, Mr. Lieutenant Governor, but Mike Hargus didn't trust you very much."

He pressed the "Play" button without waiting for an answer and the sound of two voices filled the room. The speaker built into the cassette player was small but adequate, and the voice of the man leading the taped conversation clearly belonged to Bradley Chilcott.

*"I'm telling you,"* Chilcott said on the tape, *"all we have to do is snatch that Tolliver girl and Sheridan will be putty in our hands. Killing is what he does, and once we have possession of his girlfriend's daughter, he'll have no choice but to assassinate Studds. Piece of cake. You can take that to the bank."*

Hargus seemed unconvinced. *"There's got to be a better way."*

*"We've been over this, and there is no better way,"* Chilcott insisted. *"And the plan is perfect. Studds dies, the Tolliver kid disappears forever, and we get out from under an untenable position with regard to our future."*

Jack pressed the button to stop the tape. "There's much more, of course, but I won't bore you with all the messy details. I'm sure you'll just forget them anyway, what with your memory problems and all."

Chilcott sat frozen at his desk. He stared into space with his jaw hanging open.

Jack said, "Given the fact I was such an important part of your plans, please tell me you remember me now. I'll be extremely hurt if you don't."

Bradley Chilcott deflated. He looked exactly like a life-sized balloon folding in on itself as the air was released. He hung his head, dropping it lower and lower, until it hung inches above his crossed arms on his desk.

"I can't believe that two-timing, untrustworthy son-of-a-bitch secretly recorded us without me knowing." He was mumbling and his words were hard to make out.

"I know, I know," Jack commiserated. "Sometimes it seems as though you can't trust anyone in this day and age. But look on the bright side," he added. "That's one guy who'll never double-cross you again. He's gone and he's not coming back. Not in this lifetime."

Chilcott's head dropped onto his desk and he began wheezing as he struggled to breathe.

"Asthma," he rasped weakly. "Stress induces it. I have an inhaler in my top desk drawer. Please let me unlock the drawer so I can breathe again."

Jack raised his eyebrows, amused. "By all means, Brad. Knock yourself out."

Chilcott reached into his pants pocket and pulled out a key ring.

Picked through it with trembling hands.

Found the one he was looking for and inserted the key.

Yanked the drawer open and dropped the keys on his desk.

Lifted out a Glock 19 semi-auto pistol and pointed it at Jack.

Said, "Don't think for one single second I will hesitate to use this on you, Mr. Sheridan."

His voice was suddenly clear and strong.

And filled with deadly intent.

# 42

Jack sat unmoving, legs crossed at the knee, gun still on the couch next to him.

He cleared his throat.

Smiled.

Said, "Well, this is quite the miracle cure, isn't it? I'm so glad you're feeling better. You had me quite concerned there for a minute. Sudden-onset asthma. Very serious. Very scary."

Chilcott ignored Jack's remarks. "Now you listen to me," he demanded. "You're going to hand over that tape and any others you may have, right now. Then I'm calling that policeman outside and turning you over to him. I've been assaulted in my own home and I'll not stand for it."

"You want me to hand over the tapes."

"That's right."

"The ones where you incriminate yourself, not just in a kidnapping but a murder-for-hire plot as well."

"You heard me. Do it!" Chilcott's gun hand was shaking like the weapon weighed twenty pounds, and his voice cracked from the strain of the situation.

"And if I refuse?"

"Then you die, right here and now. It's a clear case of self-defense. You broke into my home and attacked me and I had no choice but to defend myself."

Jack again pretended to consider Chilcott's words. He pursed his lips and paused a moment and then nodded. "You make a compelling case, Mr. Lieutenant Governor."

195

"I thought you might see it my way."

"But I'll have to pass."

Chilcott's face reddened and he blew out a breath angrily. "This gun is loaded," he threatened.

"I believe you."

"There's a round in the chamber."

"I believe you."

"Then what the hell is wrong with you? You don't think I have what it takes to pull this trigger? Is that it?"

"Let me ask you a question," Jack said calmly. "Do you really think I would have gone to all the trouble of outwitting your loyal bodyguard outside and breaking in here, then waiting around for hours for you to return—*hours*, Brad—without searching your office thoroughly? Without searching your *desk* thoroughly? Do you think so little of me, Brad?"

A flicker of doubt crossed Chilcott's face. "This drawer was locked," he said, thrusting his jaw out defiantly.

"So was your house, and yet here I am."

"Last chance. Eject the tape from the machine or die."

"See, the thing about your gun," Jack continued, "is that it feels the same in your hand as it always does because it *is* the same. Mostly. Same magazine, filled with 9mm rounds. It's the same weight as always, right, Brad?"

"What are you babbling about?"

"But there's one critical difference between your gun as it was when I entered this office and your gun as it is now. Would you like me to elaborate?"

Chilcott's hand was now shaking so badly he clamped his left hand on top of his right in an attempt to steady the weapon. He stared at Jack, saying nothing, his eyes large and panicked.

"You see, Brad, the thing about that gun you're holding is that I've removed the chambered round and replaced it with what's called a snap cap. Ever heard of them?"

Chilcott stared, his face turning white.

"I'll take that as a 'no.' You see, Brad, snap caps are exactly the same as standard 9mm cartridges with one critical difference: they contain no primer and no bullet. So if you pull that trigger, do you know what's going to happen?"

Still no answer.

"Nothing's going to happen. That weapon you're holding will do you no good in terms of killing me. It's of absolutely no value to you in your current situation. *My* gun, however, will still fire, and roughly a half-second after I pick it up off this couch. I'm afraid I win, Brad."

Chilcott's confusion was plain. It was obvious to Jack he didn't know enough about his weapon to know whether Jack was telling the truth or trying to con him.

Jack sighed. "Go ahead. Just pull the trigger and get this over with. We have important matters to discuss and I don't have all day."

Chilcott clamped his jaw shut and ground his teeth together. Then he jammed his finger into the trigger guard and squeezed.

*Click.*

"I told you," Jack said.

With an inarticulate groan of rage, he threw the weapon at Jack.

It sailed across the room and missed him by three feet, smashing off the wall to Jack's right and dropping harmlessly to the floor.

Jack never moved.

"Now that we understand each other," he said quietly, "allow me to place my cards on the table."

"You're going to kill me, aren't you?" Chilcott mumbled.

"No, Brad, I'm not. As much pleasure as doing do would bring me, I am not going to kill you. Probably."

A tiny glimmer of hope shone in Chilcott's eyes as he raised them to Jack's. "What's that supposed to mean?"

He smiled. "It means you're going to kill yourself."

# 43

*"What?"* Chilcott was dumbfounded. "I could never kill myself! Why in the hell would I do that?"

"At last we're getting down to business. Here's the thing, Brad. What I just played for you is a snippet from the original tape I took off Mr. Hargus's body. Unfortunately for you, there are now multiple copies of this tape out there in the world. Even as we speak, one is making its way to the editorial board of the New York Times. Another is headed to the FBI."

Chilcott's face paled further.

"Both tapes should be arriving at their destinations—" he made a show of glancing at his watch—"just about now. When that happens, I think it goes without saying your life will…change. Your political career will be over, obviously, and with you publically declawed I doubt your long-suffering wife will stick around for longer than, oh, maybe five minutes. And shortly after *that* you'll be on your way to prison."

Chilcott had closed his eyes and he rested his head heavily in his hands.

"Unless I've very badly misjudged you," Jack said, "you would rather die than suffer the kind of utter, abject humiliation in your future."

Maryland's lieutenant governor moaned, the sound low and hopeless and pathetic. But then he stopped.

Opened his eyes.

"Wait just a goddamn minute," he said. He gazed at Jack with a bit of the cunning he'd previously exhibited. "You're full of shit."

"Really. How so?"

"You can't afford to send those tapes to the authorities. You're mentioned prominently in them. Hell, you're the whole reason the tapes even exist! The minute the FBI hears your name you'll be on your way to jail just like me. Except for one critical difference. *I'll* go to Club Fed and *you'll* do hard time, because I have influential contacts and you don't."

Jack was amazed at how quickly Chilcott's entire demeanor had changed. Again. The second he'd sensed a loophole he could use to his benefit he pounced, and now he looked strong. Relatively speaking.

It was time to dash his hopes. "Please, Brad, try to keep up, will you? You're embarrassing yourself."

"What are you talking about? I'm right and you know it."

"You're not thinking things through. It's perfectly understandable, given the strain you're under, but your reasoning is faulty."

"How?" He tried to sound resolute, but some of the doubt had already begun creeping back into his voice and his demeanor.

"Think about it. I know you researched me extensively. You discussed that research at length with Hargus on the tapes. Thank you for that, by the way. I couldn't figure out how either of you had ever become aware of me, but finding out you worked at the CIA answered that question for me. I've done more than one contract job for them."

Silence.

"Anyway, given your experience in the intelligence community, I'm surprised it hasn't occurred to you that *I* might have a few contacts of my own inside the same community."

More silence, although this time when Jack glanced at him, he swallowed heavily.

"One of those contacts is an NSA employee named Ron Earl. Ron is what most people would consider a technological prodigy. Ron makes Bill Gates look like the village idiot. Ron also works for me occasionally on a contract basis, and do you know what he was able to do?"

Chilcott shook his head mutely. Jack didn't know whether the gesture was an admission that he didn't know what Ron Earl had done for him or an acknowledgement that he was well and truly fucked. Either way, Jack took the gesture as an invitation to continue.

"Mr. Earl was able to digitally remove all traces of my name from the recordings, as well as all traces of the Tolliver's names. He assures me our identities are completely unrecoverable. Now I'm no computer whiz, Brad. Between you and me, I'm lucky to get the damned thing to boot up. But when someone like Ron Earl tells me those names are gone from the tapes, I believe him.

"So," Jack continued, "when the authorities review the tapes, all they're going to hear is you convincing your chief of security to kidnap someone's daughter in order to blackmail the mother's boyfriend into assassinating Maryland Governor Jim Studds. Our names will come through as nothing more than static. White noise."

Chilcott had begun breathing heavily again and Jack hammered the final nail into the coffin.

"Wow," he said wonderingly. "Can you imagine how *that's* going to play on CNN? What a gold mine for them, Brad, am I right? They'll air those tapes over and over every hour for days. Weeks, probably. They'll devote entire programs to dissecting the information on them. And then, once your criminal trial starts, they'll do it all again. You know what vultures the media are. They're relentless. But of course you're well aware of that, aren't you, Brad?"

The lieutenant governor's eyes were wide and bloodshot and he struggled to gulp down panicked breaths.

He deserved no less.

Jack checked his watch again.

"Yeah," he said. "My guess is they'll be here to take you away sometime around seven or eight o'clock tonight. Certainly no later than nine. By eleven you'll be the lead story on every news broadcast from here to Afghanistan. And the coverage will only get more intense from there."

He smiled chummily at Chilcott, whose eyes had glazed over. He didn't appear to be listening. "That's a pretty good deal for someone who craves the spotlight as much as you. Hell, the best publicist in the world couldn't buy that kind of coverage, am I right, Brad?"

Chilcott shook his drooping head. His steel-grey politician's hair hung in a sweaty tangle over his forehead. Jack thought he could see a tendril of drool dripping down the man's chin, but it might have been a trick of the light.

"Buck up, Brad," Jack said encouragingly. "There's a way out of this."

The man seemed to have gotten very tired. He didn't move.

"*BRAD,*" Jack said sharply, and Chilcott jumped in his chair. His nerves were shot. "Listen to me and try to pay attention."

The murderous politician raised his head, slowly and only with seemingly great effort, the muscles in his neck straining. Finally he met Jack's gaze with hopeless eyes.

Jack reached into his briefcase and lifted out a small round plastic container filled with pills. He lifted the container. Displayed it to Chilcott.

"Ever heard of Carvedilol, Brad?"

No answer.

"Carvedilol is your way out of this mess, and it's far more humane than you deserve. You'll take a handful, feel a few seconds of mild to moderate chest pain, and then drift away to whatever hell awaits you after this life. You can even wash the pills down with what's left of your drink if you'd like."

Jack watched Chilcott's chest rise and fall rapidly. The man was nearly panting, and Jack thought the odds were close to fifty-fifty he would suffer a heart attack on the spot.

Jack stood and moved to the big desk.

Lifted Chilcott's hand. It was simultaneously cold and sweaty.

He uncapped the pill bottle and dropped maybe two dozen tablets into Chilcott's palm, then closed his fingers around them. The doomed man was shaking so badly, Jack wondered whether he'd be able to get them into his mouth without spilling them all over the floor.

"Take these," he demanded. "Now."

Chilcott didn't move.

"Or I shoot you in the head," Jack said. "Your decision. But our time is up. You need to make your choice."

Chilcott finally spoke, answering in a whisper. "Don't let my wife and kids find me. I can't do that to them."

Jack was ready for the request. His response was swift and harsh. "But you had no problem traumatizing someone else's child, did you?"

"Please…"

"Fortunately for you, I don't have it in me to torture your family for your mistakes. I'll be sure your body is discovered before your wife returns home with your children."

Jack had barely gotten the words out when Chilcott lifted his fist to his mouth and dumped the pills inside. He drained the glass of now watered-down scotch and sat back in his chair, refusing to meet Jack's eyes.

Jack retreated to the couch and waited for the end.

It wouldn't be long.

# 44

Carvedilol belongs to the class of medications known as Beta-blockers. Their main purpose, ironically, is for treatment of individuals with heart disease. Used properly, Beta-blockers prevent excessive stimulation of the heart muscle by slowing the heart rate.

An overdose of a Beta-blocker such as Carvedilol would induce the obvious result: the heart rate would not just slow, it would stop. Death from a dosage of Carvedilol in the amount Jack had given Chilcott would take less than five minutes.

From the couch Jack watched impassively as Chilcott choked down all the medication in two massive swallows. The politician refused to meet Jack's gaze, staring over Jack's shoulder at something, or perhaps nothing.

Within ninety seconds of swallowing the medication, Chilcott's eyes grew wider and his face paler. His chest rose and fell rapidly and his eyes darted about the room.

Still he said nothing. After all the talking he'd done on Mike Hargus's secret tape, maybe there was nothing left to say.

His body began to shake as sweat rolled down his face. Without warning he clutched at his heaving chest and dropped sideways out of his chair, nearly striking his skull on the corner of the desk.

Jack stood and moved slightly so he could see. Chilcott lay on his side, shivering like the temperature had dropped thirty degrees.

"Help…help…me…" Chilcott whispered.

"Just thought you should know something," Jack said calmly.

Chilcott's eyes focused desperately on him as he continued. "I was just kidding about sending those tapes to the FBI and the New York Times. Even if I had been successful at removing my name and those of the Tollivers from the tapes, the authorities would eventually have been able to trace us. Given your experience in the intelligence community, you really should have seen through that ruse, Brad."

Chilcott's eyes were bloodshot and glazed but he held Jack's gaze steadily, even as his head thrashed and he struggled to breathe.

"Oh, and one last thing before you go," Jack said. "You shouldn't have been so quick to throw your gun at me after firing that snap cap. The rest of the rounds in the magazine were live. You would have felt the difference in the gun's weight if I'd replaced them all. If you'd just taken a second shot, you could have blown my skull all over your wall.

"Ah, well." He shrugged and smiled. "Live and learn, right Brad?"

He returned to the couch.

Placed the mini cassette player and the remainder of the Carvedilol tablets into the briefcase and snapped it shut.

Picked the case up by the handle and craned his head to see that Bradley Chilcott had stopped struggling. His eyes were closed. Death had taken him with his face locked in an agonized grimace.

Jack moved to the prone body. He bent and felt for a pulse, first on the inside of the wrist and then on the carotid artery.

Nothing.

Chilcott was gone.

He stood and walked behind Chilcott's desk, stepping over the man's body and sweeping the floor with his eyes until locating the snap cap cartridge that had ejected from the gun when Chilcott had fired his one pointless shot. He picked it up and placed it in his pocket and smiled, picturing the investigators trying to determine why in the hell the lieutenant governor had thrown his gun at his attacker instead of firing it.

Finally he looked for the key ring Chilcott had used to open his locked desk drawer. It was on a corner of the desk, exactly where the desperate man had tossed it after removing his gun.

Jack pocketed the keys.

Shrugged into his overcoat and hat.

Lifted his briefcase and descended the stairs to the first floor.

\* \* \*

Bradley Chilcott's car was a midnight blue Ford Thunderbird. It was one of the retro models from a few years ago, manufactured to look old but in reality completely modern. The car was exactly like Bradley Chilcott, flashy and conspicuous.

Jack picked through the keys until locating the right one. He could have hotwired the car, but why bother?

A garage door opener remote was affixed to the sun visor and Jack pressed the button. He started the car as the door rumbled upward on its tracks. Outside, the rain continued to fall, pelting the ground in a cold spray.

Good. The weather should help facilitate his escape.

He wondered briefly whether the lieutenant governor's movements were being coordinated with the Annapolis Police for the benefit of the patrol officer parked outside.

He doubted the authorities would go to that much trouble in the absence of a specific threat against Chilcott but couldn't be certain.

Hopefully the heavy rain plus the element of surprise would combine to prevent a confrontation that could get messy. Jack backed the car down the driveway and eased into the road. He couldn't make out any details of the officer's appearance behind the police cruiser's windshield, which of course meant the officer couldn't tell for sure that it wasn't Bradley Chilcott behind the wheel of his car.

Hopefully.

Jack raised a hand in salute to the officer—a salute that wasn't returned—and accelerated slowly away. He kept his eyes glued to the rearview mirror as he signaled for a left turn, waiting to see whether the cruiser pulled away from the curb and began to follow.

It didn't.

Good. Jack had no desire to injure an innocent police officer, not to mention deal with the shitstorm an altercation with law enforcement would bring.

He rounded the corner and drove out of sight of the sentry.

Seconds later he arrived at his rental.

He pulled to the curb and exited Chilcott's car, leaving the keys in the ignition and the vehicle unlocked.

He climbed behind the wheel of the rental and drove off in a direction opposite the police officer and the now-dead lieutenant governor's home, heading for the freeway and the auto rental agency.

As he drove, he picked up his burner phone and punched in the number he'd used earlier to report the suspicious package to the Annapolis Police.

The dispatcher answered, again on the second ring, and Jack began speaking immediately. "Listen carefully, because I'm only going to say this once. Lieutenant Governor Bradley Chilcott has suffered a massive heart attack inside his home. He's dead."

"Who is this?"

"I'm not finished yet," Jack said sharply. "Pay attention. The lieutenant governor's final wish was that his family—particularly his children—not be the ones to find his body. Please send the appropriate medical personnel to his home address immediately, as his family is due home within the hour. Do you understand everything I've told you?"

"Sir, you're going to have to tell me your name. Right now. And how are you getting your information? Are you with Lieutenant Governor Chilcott?"

Jack disconnected the call. He drove up the ramp to Interstate 97, which would take him to I-95 North toward Baltimore. His hope was that no one in Chilcott's neighborhood had taken note of the nondescript Ford Focus rental during the short time it was parked around the corner from Chilcott's home, but the possibility that someone *had* was one reason he'd chosen a rental agency located more than ten miles from Annapolis.

There was no reason to make the authorities' job easy.

Even if someone had jotted down the license plate number of the Focus, the situation would be chaotic at the Chilcott residence. It would take time to determine just what the hell had happened, and before the neighborhood had been canvassed for witnesses, Jack would long since have returned the car to the agency.

Once that happened it wouldn't matter if the car were traced. Jack's forged driver's licenses and credit cards, provided by The Organization to their operators upon request and with no questions asked, were sophisticated enough to fool even the most suspicious examiner.

The documents, of course, would lead nowhere. The trail into the mysterious man who'd rented three separate cars over the course of three consecutive days would turn colder than a New Hampshire winter. Jack had been sure to wear a baseball cap pulled low on his head to obscure his face from the ubiquitous CCTV cameras during his transactions, which meant identification would be impossible with only the grainy, black and white footage to go on.

Less than twenty minutes after Bradley Chilcott's sudden— and as far as Jack was concerned, unlamented—death, Jack had returned the rental.

Less than fifteen minutes after that, he'd briskly walked the three-quarters of a mile to the parking lot in which he'd left his truck.

Barely half an hour after pouring the Carvedilol into Bradley Chilcott's shaking hand Jack was in his truck, moving steadily north on I-95.

# 45

There was no real reason to stay another night in the Baltimore/ Washington area. Jack was wired, as he was upon the completion of every job. He could easily have driven the eight to ten hours home without any concerns about falling asleep at the wheel. Even after dealing with rush-hour traffic delays early in the evening he'd have been home by three a.m.

But that kind of timing didn't work for Jack. He wanted to be back in New Hampshire at a particular time, and for a particular reason.

So when he reached a point halfway between Washington and Philadelphia on the interstate, Jack found a cheap, anonymous roadside motel, the kind of place he was most comfortable in, the kind of place that accepted cash and asked few questions.

He slept well and was back on the road before sunrise.

# 46

When the call came in on her cell phone, Edie briefly considered ignoring it.

But only briefly.

She'd been thinking almost nonstop about Jack Sheridan since leaving him standing alone and miserable in his driveway four days ago. She'd watched him in her rearview mirror as she drove away, his shoulders slumped and his hands jammed into his pockets.

He hadn't called or come around since, a request she'd asked him to honor but one she now found herself second-guessing.

She missed him.

She missed his gentle manner and his corny jokes and the way he smiled when he looked at her. *Every single time* he looked at her.

And she missed the way he treated Janie. Not like a father, not exactly, but as the kind of role model a young girl needed from a man: strong and calm and caring. He was never too busy to stop what he was doing and listen intently to the seven-year-old's stories, as if her words were the most important thing in the world to him at that moment.

It was all so damned confusing. How the *hell* could she even consider a professional assassin the kind of role model she wanted for her child? How the *hell* could she consider a professional assassin a suitable partner for herself?

How?

She didn't know the answers to those questions. She didn't know whether there even *were* answers to those questions. But they'd been on her mind constantly. From the moment she woke up in the morning until the moment she finally drifted off to sleep at night—and sleep hadn't come easily since Janie's kidnapping—those issues were practically all she thought about. Between confusion about her relationship with Jack and worry about any lingering effects of the kidnapping and subsequent rescue on Janie's psyche, it *was* all she thought about.

So when her cell phone buzzed, her hesitation had been almost—not quite, but almost—nonexistent. She picked up and felt the familiar butterflies in her stomach at the sound of his voice, the butterflies she'd experienced when she first started dating in high school and that she'd been convinced she would never feel again until she'd met Jack.

She kept her voice noncommittal, though.

Cool.

Distant.

"Hello, Jack."

"Hi, Edie. How are you and Janie doing?"

"We're fine." She worked to keep her voice emotionless.

"I'm glad. Listen, Edie…"

"Yes?"

"I've been out of town for a couple of days. I'm driving up I-93 now and I was hoping maybe I could stop by the diner and we could talk. You know, just for a few minutes."

She hesitated. She was still hurt and confused but she knew one thing with utter certainty: Jack Sheridan would have given his life—without hesitation or regret—to get Janie back, and that the only way he would have been denied in that quest would have been if he'd been killed trying.

And her workday at the diner *was* almost finished.

Janie had insisted on going back to school the day after her return from that awful cottage on Lake Winnipesaukee. Edie considered her desire to resume a normal routine a positive sign, but at the same time she wasn't about to allow her only child to walk home to an empty house like she'd done on the afternoon of the kidnapping, even if it was in the middle of the day.

Yes, she had to keep the diner up and running. As her only source of income, it was critical she not allow her focus to slip. And yes, running a small business required a herculean effort and major investment of time.

But her business was her business.

Her child was her life.

So every day since Jack had recovered Janie, Edie left the diner in the capable hands of her head chef at three o'clock and drove to Edie's school. She picked up her daughter, chauffeured her home and they spent the rest of the day together.

Janie had already begun complaining that she wanted to go back to the way things had been before the kidnapping, that it was embarrassing to be picked up at school every day like a baby. Edie couldn't help but consider that another positive sign, but she also wasn't prepared to approve that kind of request.

Not yet.

She glanced at her watch. Two-fifteen. There was really no good reason she couldn't spare a few minutes for Jack.

But it was so soon, and the wound on her heart was still open and raw and sore, and she was still so confused.

This was a very small town, though, and it was inevitable she would bump into Jack Sheridan. A lot. Even if he stopped eating at the Three Squares, their paths would cross at the grocery store or the drugstore or the town's only movie theatre. The odds of going more than a few days at a time without them seeing each other were slim.

They would have to talk eventually. Maybe it would be best to get the awkwardness out of the way, rather than letting it build and fester. Maybe a few minutes spent in conversation now would allow them to reach some sort of understanding, even if Edie had no earthly idea what that understanding might be.

And she missed him so much.

That was what it all boiled down to, really. She could rationalize agreeing to see him, tell herself it would be the wise choice to make for all the sensible reasons in the world, but the essence of the matter was simple: *she missed him.*

She checked her watch again and realized it had been a long time since anyone had spoken. The phone was still pressed to her ear but no one was saying anything. She could just make out the rumble of Jack's truck's engine in the background, but he was being patient, allowing her to work through the issues he knew she was dealing with.

"Okay," she said, as if there had been any doubt. "I'll meet you. But only for a few minutes. I have to leave soon to pick up Janie at school."

"Of course. And thank you. I'm turning off the highway now, so I'll be at the diner in less than ninety seconds."

She spoke brusquely. "That's fine. But I don't want to do it inside the diner. It's hard enough dealing with well-intentioned questions from my coworkers and all the customers who know we're...who know we *were*...together, without making the situation worse by sharing a booth as if nothing's changed."

"I understand." His voice stayed even, but Edie could sense the pain behind the words and she felt a momentary flash of savage satisfaction. *See? I can hurt you, too.*

Then shame replaced satisfaction and she softened her tone. "I'll be in the parking lot when you get here and I'll join you in your truck. Is that okay?"

"That'll be fine, Edie. Whatever you're comfortable with is fine by me."

"I'll see you in a minute." She thumbed the button to disconnect the call and closed her eyes. She felt exhausted.

# 47

Jack spotted Edie the moment he turned into the Three Squares parking lot. She stood just outside the front entrance, arms crossed over her chest as she leaned against the side of the building. Her shaggy blonde hair just reached her shoulders, which were hunched as if protecting her from a cold wind.

But the weather was perfect. Blue skies and warm sunshine.

They exchanged noncommittal waves and Jack nosed the truck into a space. By the time he'd killed the engine she was there. She opened the passenger door and climbed into his truck, looking like salvation and smelling like lavender.

And Jack's heart broke a little more.

Edie said, "Hey, stranger."

"You got that right." Jack smiled. "They don't come any stranger than me."

"So…you're returning home from a 'business trip.'"

"Yep."

"Business."

Jack nodded. "Business. You don't have to worry about Janie falling victim to kidnappings or assassination plots ever again. At least not from the two lunatics behind this past week's madness. The issue has officially become moot."

As Jack watched, Edie visibly relaxed. Her slim frame seemed to melt into the seat. She took a deep breath, held it for a moment, and then blew it out in a calming sigh.

Then she cleared her throat. "I don't understand what you do.

You already know that. But thank you for protecting my little girl. She's my whole life and I don't think I could ever have been comfortable again if…"

She had begun to cry softly. The urge to slide over and take her in his arms and hold and protect her was visceral and almost overwhelming.

But she was no longer his to hold or protect. She'd made that clear. So he stayed where he was.

"How's Janie holding up?" he asked.

She brushed the back of one small hand across her eyes and looked down as if the floor of Jack's truck was the most fascinating thing she'd ever seen.

She sighed. "Janie asks about you every day. She wants to know why we haven't been doing 'fun stuff' anymore like we used to."

"What do you tell her?"

Finally she raised her eyes to his. "That's just it, Jack. I don't know what to say. How can I answer her questions when *I* don't know what to think?"

He nodded. "It was a mistake for me to become involved, given the obvious risks attached. I've known how chancy it would be to get close to someone since I made the choice to continue the only real occupation I've ever had after leaving the military, the only thing I've ever been good at. And for that I apologize, but—"

"You still don't get it, Jack. That wasn't your mistake. Your mistake was in not trusting me enough to make my own decisions about my life and the life of my child. Your mistake was in not opening up and sharing such a major part of *your* life with the woman you claimed to care about. I fell in love with you, Jack, and then I discovered the man I had fallen in love with was a stranger!"

For a moment no one spoke.

Then Jack said, "I've quit The Organization. On my way to Maryland I met with my contact and told him I was finished. This nasty little business I just concluded was my last job."

Edie stared, mouth hanging open, eyes wet with tears.

"Jack," she whispered. "I don't—"

"I've been considering quitting for a long time, Edie. And I know how it looks, like this is some pathetic attempt to get you back. I don't blame you for thinking that. But that's not it. Not completely, at least," he said with a bitter laugh.

"But you just said your job is more like a calling, that it's the only career you've ever had."

"And that's true as far as it goes. But what I do…it's not an occupation that's conducive to a long career, Edie. I'm old by operator standards. My back is creaky, my bones ache all the time, my reflexes aren't what they once were. It's time for me to move on to something else. It's past time, really."

"But…" She shook her head and shrugged. "What will you do?"

"I'll find something. That's a concern for another day. Right now I just want to chat with you and then go home and sleep for about three days straight."

Edie glanced at the clock on Jack's dashboard. Sighed deeply. "I've got to go. I have to pick Janie up at school."

She reached for the door handle and Jack blurted, "I miss you."

She had stopped crying for a moment but now the tears resumed, twin trails of heartbreak rolling down her cheeks. This time she made no effort to hide them. "I miss you, too."

"Maybe we could start over. They say there are no second chances in life, but why not? Who made up that rule, and what the hell do they know, anyway? We'll start slow. See what happens. Maybe a casual dinner, just you, me, and Janie. No expectations, no strings attached. One meal."

Her right hand had frozen on the handle, but now she opened the door and slipped down onto the pavement.

Looked back into the truck, squinting against the sunlight's glare.

"I don't know, Jack. I just don't know."

She closed the door with a thunk.

Turned and walked toward her car.

She never looked back.

# EPILOGUE

The man stepped out of his Jaguar, fedora tilted forward at a jaunty angle. He wasn't making a fashion statement. He was simply hiding his identity, and the way he wore his headgear accomplished that goal quite effectively.

He had parked in one of the most dangerous neighborhoods in Lawrence, Massachusetts. It was an area filled with drugs and crime and blight and hopelessness. He would seem a natural target in these surroundings, a fool with more money than brains, a guy living on borrowed time who would be jumped and relieved of his wallet and his expensive watch at the first opportunity.

But the man wasn't worried.

This wasn't his first time in the neighborhood.

Nor was it his first experience making the short walk from his car's unobtrusive parking space into what appeared to be an abandoned brick building. The structure was a crumbling relic of a bygone era, invisible and ignored, awaiting the wrecking ball.

But looks could be deceiving, especially in this area.

The building was not abandoned, and the man had been here many times over the past several years.

He entered through a rear door that looked decrepit but was in fact heavily reinforced. Just inside the doorway he was met by a muscular Hispanic man of indeterminate age wearing sunglasses and a skin-tight t-shirt, with an ugly black pistol strapped to his waist. The man frisked him quickly but thoroughly and then waved him on with the bored expression of someone who'd been doing his job for a very long time.

In no other circumstance would the man in the fedora put up with the rough treatment he received at the hands of the Hispanic guard, but these were not typical circumstances. He received the same treatment every time he came here but never became upset or angry. He understood the need for caution and appreciated it. He still didn't like it.

He climbed the stairs to a viewing area that had been constructed just for him. It was Spartan and cramped, and consisted of a small round table, a couple of mismatched wooden chairs, a recliner that had probably been new about the time the man in the fedora graduated law school, and a small TV with a DVD player set up next to it. There was a minimally stocked bar. Ancient copies of Penthouse magazine were strewn randomly around the viewing area.

It was decidedly low-tech.

It was dirty and uncomfortable.

The man in the fedora loved it here. This was the one place in the entire world he could come and truly be himself.

*　*　*

The evening's entertainment was a little late getting started, so the man in the fedora passed the time watching DVDs of previous shows. He mixed a strong drink and sat back in the recliner and rubbed himself languidly through his trousers as the action unfolded on the screen.

Then the sound of a door being shoved open downstairs signaled that the live performance was about to begin. The man in the fedora rose quickly and positioned himself in one of the mismatched wooden chairs, dragging it to the balcony railing for an unrestricted view.

Below, two men flanked a third, dragging/pushing/carrying him to a heavy wooden chair that had been set up precisely in the middle of the room. The victim wore a police officer's uniform and a blindfold, and he had been gagged. The two men—they were heavily muscled, like the guard at the doorway, and looked to be in their mid-to-late twenties—dropped the cop roughly into the chair and in seconds had secured his ankles to the chair legs and his wrists to the chair's arms.

They strode to the door and exited the room, returning almost immediately with the supplies that would drive the show: a small metal trash can and a set of sturdy-looking gardening shears with long wooden handles and a heavy iron cutting jaw. They placed the trashcan next to the chair and aligned it with the right armrest, to which the cop's wrist had been securely affixed.

The shears they set on the floor next to the trashcan, on a section of grey concrete that had been stained rust brown.

Then the two men left the room once more.

This time when they returned, they were accompanied by three nervous-looking males, all of whom looked young. Shockingly young. One was black, one was white and one appeared Hispanic.

The men in charge lined the three young boys up against the far wall. One stood with them while the other approached the police officer and removed his blindfold and then his gag.

The minute the gag came out the cop started talking, telling them they were making a mistake, that assaulting a police officer was a very bad idea but that they hadn't gone so far they couldn't still fix things, that it wasn't too late to simply let him go, and that if they did so the consequences would be minimal.

The man who'd removed the blindfold and gag shut the cop up by punching him in the face. The cop's head snapped back and a sickening *crack* signified a broken, probably shattered, nose, and blood spurted and began running down the cop's face and flowing onto his uniform shirt.

But he stopped talking.

The man who had punched the cop surveyed the three kids lined up against the wall like a junior high gym teacher picking out the next student to shimmy up the rope.

After a moment's thoughtful consideration he selected the white kid. Pointed at him and called him forward silently, rotating his hand until it was palm-up and then bending the fingers at the third knuckles in the universal "come here" gesture.

The kid looked liked he would rather be anywhere else in the world. But he stepped forward without hesitation. He clearly knew what was coming and he was shaking, the man in the fedora could see it from his viewing perch all the way across the room and up one level.

The man in the fedora was nearly shaking as well, but it was from arousal, not fear, and he could feel himself getting hard again in his trousers. Seeing the terror of the recruits was almost as exciting as seeing the actual ceremony, which was about to take place.

"Do it," the older man said to the white kid, and then he stepped away, moving a few feet in the direction of the other two recruits and the second group leader. He stopped and waited impassively for what would come next, arms crossed behind his back.

The cop was moaning and bleeding heavily from the face, but now he started babbling again. His voice was thick from his ruined nose and all the blood he continued to swallow, and any semblance of the authoritative manner he'd previously attempted to project was long gone.

He begged for mercy.

Begged the kid to stop.

And for a moment he did. The kid had reached reluctantly for the shears and now he stood uncertainly, bony arms holding the gardening tool at his side as the cop continued to urge him to reconsider what he was about to do.

Finally the older man shook his head in disgust. He muttered something that the man in the fedora could not quite make out and then stepped forward. He jammed the gag back into the cop's mouth and secured it and the cop thrashed wildly in his seat, his ability to breathe through his rapidly swelling nose nearly nonexistent.

The group leader let him struggle for a moment and then yanked the gag back out. Before the cop could say anything the group leader rasped, "Not one more word. You say one word, just one, and the gag goes back in and stays in, do you understand me?"

The cop panted, gulping wide mouthfuls of air, and for a moment the man in the fedora thought he hadn't heard the group leader. Then he nodded tiredly. With each downward motion of his head large droplets of blood splattered onto his shirt, which was now soaked and stained.

The kid with the shears looked like he might be about to cry, but the older man whispered something to him and he nodded.

The older man grabbed the cop's right hand and forced his fingers widely apart as the kid opened the jaws of the gardening shears and thrust them around the cop's pinkie finger. The kid was shaking badly and the man in the fedora could see he'd opened up a deep gash on the cop's knuckles.

But that would soon be the least of the cop's problems.

It already was.

The cop tried to struggle, but he had no leverage and the group leader was incredibly strong. His arms were massive and he'd performed this ritual many times and by now had it down to a science. The group leader held the cop's hand motionless between the jaws of the shears.

He looked up and nodded to the kid.

The man in the fedora watched, breathless, waiting for the show to continue.

And then it did.

Jack Sheridan will return soon in his third pulp thriller. To be the first to learn about new releases, and for the opportunity to win free ebooks, signed copies of print books, and other swag, take a moment to sign up for Allan Leverone's email newsletter at AllanLeverone.com.

Reader reviews are hugely important to authors looking to set their work apart from the competition. If you have a moment to spare, please consider taking a moment to leave a brief, honest review of *Trigger Warning* at Amazon's *Trigger Warning* page, at Goodreads, or at your favorite review site, and thank you.

# Acknowledgements

Special thanks to Joe Serafino for taking the time and effort to help make my showdown scene between Jack Sheridan and Bradley Chilcott as dramatic—and yet still realistic—as possible. Joe's gun knowledge is as extensive as it is invaluable, a resource I've mined more than once and one for which I'm extremely grateful to him for sharing with me.

The cover art for *Trigger Warning* was designed and rendered by Kealan Patrick Burke of Elderlemon Design. Kealan's a talented and award-winning author in his own right who also has been doubly blessed with incredible design skills. His work is recognizable yet unique, providing the perfect ambience to the Jack Sheridan Pulp Thriller series before the reader ever opens the book.

Last but definitely not least, I want to thank you, the reader. I was in my fifties before my first book was published, and all those decades of life—and reading—have given me plenty of perspective. I'm well aware you have about a zillion other options on which to spend your free time and your money, and I am humbled and eternally grateful that you've chosen to spend a little of that time and money with my work.

Thank you. I'll never take you for granted.

# Also from Allan Leverone

## Thrillers

*The Organization: A Jack Sheridan Pulp Thriller*
*The Lonely Mile*
*Final Vector*
*Parallax View: A Tracie Tanner Thriller*
*All Enemies: A Tracie Tanner Thriller*
*The Omega Connection: A Tracie Tanner Thriller*
*The Hitler Deception: A Tracie Tanner Thriller*
*The Kremlyov Infection: A Tracie Tanner Thriller*

## Horrow/Dark Thrillers

*Mr. Midnight*
*After Midnight*
*Paskagankee*
*Revenant: A Paskagankee Novel Book Two*
*Wellspring: A Paskagankee Novel Book Three*
*Grimoire: A Paskagankee Novel Book Four*
*Covenant*
*Linger: Mark of the Beast (Written with Edward Fallon)*

## Horrow

*The Becoming*
*Flight 12: A Kristin Cunningham Thriller*

## Story Collections

*Postcards from the Apocalypse*
*Uncle Brick and the Four Novelettes*
*Letters from the Asylum: Three Complete Novellas*
*The Tracie Tanner Collection: Three Complete Thriller Novels*